TEETH OF THE WOLF

TEETH
OF
THE
WOLF

Alain Paris

Translated by
Martin Sokolinsky

HOLT, RINEHART *and* WINSTON
New York

Published in the United States in 1983 by
Holt, Rinehart and Winston, 383 Madison Avenue,
New York, New York 10017.
Published simultaneously in Canada by Holt, Rinehart and
Winston of Canada, Limited.
Originally published in France under the title *Le Commando des
salopards*.

Library of Congress Cataloging in Publication Data
Paris, Alain.
Teeth of the wolf.
Translation of: Le commando des salopards.
I. Title.
PQ2676.A699C613   1983   843'.914   83-96
ISBN 0-03-059899-0

First Edition

Designer: *Debra L. Moloshok*

Printed in the United States of America
1 3 5 7 9 10 8 6 4 2

ISBN 0-03-059899-0

Heaven help us if
we lose this war!

—Hermann Göring, after
the British ultimatum,
7:00 A.M., September 3, 1939

TEETH OF THE WOLF

1

APRIL 20, 1945, 6:30 A.M.

A distant rumble announced the prelude to the assault on that final objective—Berlin.

Marshal Zhukov's eight thousand field guns, with roughly as many "Stalin organs" and mortars, unleashed a storm of fire. As the ground shook under the battering of this mass of artillery, flashes of lightning tore rents in the mist shrouding the Prussian dawn.

Less than eighty kilometers northeast of Berlin stood Karinhall in all its audacious splendor. The huge estate, a megalomaniac's dream, was the culmination of a golden life. Unfortunately for its owner, Reichsmarschall Hermann Göring, the Führer's legal heir, the days of splendor were numbered. The Red Army, massed on the banks of the Spree, was impatiently awaiting the signal to surge forward and plunder.

Parked outside Karinhall's high iron fence were twenty-four Horch trucks covered with camouflage netting. The Luftwaffe emblem appeared on the cab door of each vehicle. Twenty-four motors idled quietly while twenty-four nervous-looking drivers waited tensely for the signal to pull out. A dozen motorcyclists, who would escort the trucks, sat on the saddles of their Zundapp K-750 machines. All eyes were fixed on the corpulent man who stood stiffly facing the fence. In an almost theatrical silence he contemplated the landscaped terraces, the wings and buttresses of the Renaissance castle, the groves of ancient trees.

The Reichsmarschall turned away slowly. Then, with an air of reluctance, he walked over to the convoy of trucks. He spoke a few words to the lead motorcyclist, who nodded solemnly, then stood back as the motors revved and the convoy lurched forward. As he watched the line of trucks grind away down the road, Hermann Göring let out a long sigh of relief: the trucks contained his silver, his works of art, the priceless treasures for which he had ransacked the museums and private collections of conquered Europe.

The last of the trucks disappeared and silence descended again on Karinhall. Göring crossed the road, moving more briskly now, and the Luftwaffe Engineer Lieutenant, standing at attention by the fence, stiffened. With an awkward gesture of his right hand the young officer indicated the detonator lying on the ground. Göring's moonlike, womanish face, which had been expressionless, puckered, and he sniffed faintly.

"Ah well," the Reichsmarschall said, "it's the kind of thing a man has to do—once in a lifetime."

Then he lifted his foot, as if about to mount a step, and pressed it firmly, unhesitatingly down on the plunger.

For a moment, nothing happened. Then, with a reverberating crash, Karinhall exploded. Six officers, and a little knot of local villagers, saw Göring's palace reduced to rubble in an instant.

There was a curious look of satisfaction on Göring's face as he removed his foot from the detonator, as if he had derived some childish gratification from the big bang. As swiftly as his bulk allowed, he walked to his official Mercedes. The running board squeaked under his weight as he stepped onto it. He paused for a moment, half in and half out of the car, and glanced back at the gutted wings and façade of Karinhall; then he heaved himself into the back of the car, slammed the door violently, and sank back into the tawny leather upholstery. He barked an order at his chauffeur. Time was pressing. At half-past eleven he had to be in Berlin for the most important reception of the year. It was Adolf Hitler's birthday.

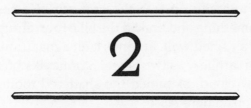

2

APRIL 27, 1945, 2:45 P.M.

Karl-Heinz Hellmann was light-headed with fatigue. For weeks he had existed in a trance, as if drugged or mildly drunk, his perceptions heightened, his energy drawn from some mysterious source outside himself.

His life had taken on the quality of a dream, and his dreams, when he managed to snatch a few hours of shallow sleep, were merely a slightly distorted continuation of his life.

As the Kettenkraftrad lurched and jolted through the craters and rubble of Potsdamerstrasse, Hellmann felt a delicious lethargy stealing through him, in spite of the intense cold and the crazy bucking of the motorcycle tractor. Because of it, perhaps. It was like being rocked in a cradle. However, this was not the time or the place to give in to sleep. He forced his eyes open and fished a cigarette out of a pocket of his hooded coat. The wheels of the Kettenkraftrad plunged into a shell hole and the cigarette slipped from his numbed fingers. He shrugged and was about to bend down to retrieve the cigarette when the vehicle skidded wildly and his head struck the iron guardrail.

"Sorry, Captain," the driver shouted above the clatter of the motor. He wore a ragged, grease-stained leather helmet. His face was haggard, his eyes bloodshot. He was glancing uneasily up into the gray sky. He seemed to decide something and braked the bike to an abrupt halt in the lee of a ruined wall. Seconds later a roar drowned out the distant artillery as two Soviet Stormoviks spewed out of the low cloud, skimmed the shattered rooftops, and strafed Potsdamerstrasse.

The driver instinctively ducked as the long brown wings swept overhead. Hellmann, pulling a fresh cigarette from his pocket, felt the downdraft of the Stormoviks' engines, and waited for the fighters to drone away before lighting his cigarette.

The driver said: "Shit."

Hellmann shrugged, and with a gesture of his cigarette, indicated the driver's battered headgear.

4

"Afrika Korps?"

The driver smiled, revealing a mouthful of blackened stumps. "Yes, sir. I made the big safari. Sollum, El Agheila, El Alamein. The good old days."

"Ah—the good old days."

The driver was about to say something when the twin roars of the returning Stormoviks made his head whip round. Simultaneously, anti-aircraft guns near the station opened fire. The Soviet planes swept back down Potsdamerstrasse, flying higher, and suddenly one of them disintegrated in a ball of fire. Vaguely, Hellmann heard the driver mutter, "Good shooting," but Hellmann was not looking at the man, or even at the black smudge in the sky. He was staring at the burned-out buildings and blackened trees of the once elegant avenue, the driver's casual phrase—"the good old days"—echoing and reechoing in his head, like a tune. It was as if he were viewing the ruins of his native city for the first time. And for some strange reason he was not remembering the good times, the heady friendships and intense love affairs of his student days, or the golden year of the Olympics when Berlin had seemed to be the center of the world. No. He was thinking about the Englishman with the unpronounceable name, Ffoulkes-Jones—Fuchs-Jonesh the boys had called him—a tall, gangling man in a tweed jacket, who would pace the avenues and boulevards of Berlin after dark, like a predatory stork, jingling the coins in his trouser pockets, looking for boys. He remembered the sour smell of Fuchs-Jonesh's body, the texture of his skin, like a plucked chicken. And his own father, with tears in his eyes, folding into his wallet Fuchs-Jonesh's dollars and pounds that meant the difference between subsistence and starvation and saying: "Your mother must never know, Karl. Never."

5

Hellmann pulled his goggles over his eyes and signaled to the driver. The driver gunned his engine and the Kettenkraftrad lurched forward. As they turned into Potsdamerplatz it halted again to make way for a column of marching soldiers. There were about fifty of them, in mud-splattered coats, under the command of six SS officers. As the column came abreast, Hellmann saw that it was composed half of old veterans of the Volkssturm, toothless pensioners barely capable of carrying their clumsy First World War rifles—as redundant as themselves—and half of Hitlerjugend, boys of twelve or thirteen, staggering under the weight of Panzerfausts, the only weapons capable of piercing the armor of the Soviet T-34 tanks.

Hellmann caught the driver's eye. The veteran of Sollum and Alamein spat deliberately, eloquently.

"Proceed," Hellmann said.

They turned the corner by the Chancellery and started down Voss-strasse. Home Guard units were poking through the ruins, searching for bodies, dead or alive. Hellmann was astonished at his own lack of emotion. These proofs of Germany's collapse—old men and boys being herded off to die uselessly; Berlin, the capital of Europe, being pounded to dust—should have made him angry, disgusted, vengeful—something. But he felt nothing.

At the next corner, almost opposite the shattered walls of the Propaganda Ministry, there was a Feldgendarmerie roadblock. Hellmann sighed. Military police. The useless busybodies of every battlefield from Marathon to Waterloo.

"Identity and unit, Herr Captain."

The MP's uniform looked freshly pressed. His voice was crisp, officious, his eyes cold.

Not troubling to disguise his boredom and disgust,

6

Hellmann pulled a sheaf of tattered papers from a pocket and handed them over.

"You are with General Wenck's Twelfth Army?"

Hellmann detected suspicion and hostility in the MP's tone. He didn't give a damn. He had his ace of trumps in another pocket.

"The front line is along the Elbe, between Zerbst, Schönebeck, and Magdeburg. That's where the fighting is, Herr Captain. How is it then that you are in Berlin?"

Hellmann was about to reply that he was on temporary attachment to GHQ, Berlin, when there were shouts and a volley of curses. He raised himself in his seat. A knot of MPs was forcing a young lieutenant toward a streetlamp. The lieutenant—he couldn't have been more than nineteen or twenty—was yelling incoherently. The MPs slipped a rope round his neck, hooked one end over the streetlamp, and hauled him aloft. There was laughter as the boy kicked and choked.

Hellmann turned away, relieved to feel rage surging through him. He noticed that his driver's face was pallid and moist, like suet.

"I have been attached to GHQ, Berlin."

The MP smiled. He pointed to the figure now dangling limply from the streetlamp. "That was his story too. He had civilian clothes concealed in his knapsack. A deserter."

Hellmann said nothing—deliberately. His silence seemed to infuriate the MP. He waved Hellmann's papers.

"You have no pass."

"I have." Hellmann paused. Then: "You wish to see it?"

The MP was at a loss for a reply. He snapped his fingers. Slowly, Hellmann brought out his pass. He watched the MP carefully as he read the document. He saw the muscles in the man's sallow face clench as the signature at the foot of the paper hit him.

Bormann.

Hellmann extended his hand and snapped his fingers, imitating the MP. The man handed him Bormann's pass, a shadow of fear in his eyes.

"May I proceed now?" Hellmann asked. "Or do you wish to delay me further?"

The MP muttered something vaguely apologetic.

Hellmann gestured toward the streetlamp.

"In a way he was lucky," he said. "The Feldgendarmerie treats deserters with greater mercy than the Russians treat prisoners. I expect you'll discover that for yourself before very long."

Then he jerked his head at his driver.

"Move."

3

As Hellmann was passing through the last roadblock separating him from the command post of Nazi resistance in besieged Berlin, there was frantic activity at 8 Prinz-Albrechtstrasse.

The Soviets' systematic bombardment had leveled or

gutted the rest of the district but, by some perverse miracle, Gestapo Headquarters was still standing. The main door of the Reich Security Administration building was wide open and a constant stream of orderlies, secretaries, and officers moved up and down the stone staircase, carrying armloads of files into the central courtyard, where a bonfire was burning.

Armed with pitchforks and rakes, four sweating soldiers were tending the fire, supervised by a detail of SS men whose duty was to ensure that every file was consigned to the blaze and that no half-charred papers fluttered over the courtyard wall. From time to time the SS officer in charge barked an order and the soldiers poked up the fire or pushed an unburnt file back into the flames. Lit at dawn, the pyre had been burning steadily ever since, the teams of record burners being relieved every two hours.

Every room, every corridor, every stairway of the building was in a state of pandemonium. Shouts, orders, and curses mingled with bursts of frantic conversation, the slamming of doors, and endlessly ringing telephones. The red carpets in the corridors, littered with cigarette butts, were burned in places. Mud had been tracked over the main staircase and over parquet floors. Water from burst pipes was staining the walls, dripping from ceilings.

At the end of the corridor on the second floor was a half-dismantled office. Its sole occupant sat on the edge of his desk, the telephone receiver pressed to his ear as he concentrated on the voice at the other end of the line. Occasionally he said "Yes" or "Understood," and then a click announced the end of the call. He set the receiver down, rose, and walked to the smoke-grimed window. He stood there for a time, lost in thought, watching thick black smoke mushroom from the buildings across the street. His breath condensed on the windowpane, and he moved a pace to the right.

There was a discreet knock at the door.

"Come in."

Slowly, he turned and stared at the dispatch rider standing stiffly in the doorway.

"A message from the Chancellery."

The courier held up a brown manila envelope.

"Hand it over."

"I have orders to deliver it to Obersturmführer Wrack personally."

"I am Obersturmführer Wrack."

The courier hesitated, then handed over the envelope, saluted, and hurried away. Wrack weighed the envelope in his hand for a moment before taking a letter opener from his desk. As he moved back to the window, he slit open the envelope and tore the official seal. Page by page, he held the Hellmann file up to the leaden light, his eye skimming over the details. *Born September 25, 1915, Berlin. Son of Hellmann, Franz-Joseph, teacher of languages, and Laupheim, Baroness Maria von. One sister. Degree in English, Friedrich Wilhelm University. Enlisted Wehrmacht (infantry) 1938. Officer Candidate School, 1940. NOTE: Unlisted in National Socialist Party.*

Wrack snorted faintly at that and turned to the next page.

British Corps Archives. Allgemeine SS Central Office. Card No. 37-A. Hellmann, Karl-Heinz. Height: 1.85. Weight: 88.45. Color of eyes: brown. Color of hair: light brown. Special marks: scar under lower lip . . .

And so on, and so on. Wrack read the character analysis perfunctorily, noting that Hellmann's sexual preferences were recorded as normal. *No outward sign of homosexuality.* He flipped impatiently through the rest of the file until he came to the photograph. He had once attended a course of lectures by an expert in physiognomy, a protégé of Himmler's; faces interested Wrack.

He studied Hellmann's face in the photograph. Good-looking. Handsome, one would have to say. A gentleman's face.

Wrack, who despised anything (or anyone) smacking of gentility, knew at once that he would dislike Hellmann, that Hellmann would have to be watched most carefully. The cast of his features was typical officer-intellectual class, the class that bred traitors and cowards.

Wrack slipped the papers back into the envelope, and slid the envelope into an inside pocket of his field jacket. Then, meticulously, he rechecked that every last scrap of paper had been removed from the drawers of his desk. Satisfied, he left the room, closing the door carefully behind him.

4

Gloves in hand, the hood of his field-gray coat raised, Hellmann watched the Kettenkraftrad drive away. Instantly he felt lonely, cut off. There had been something reassuring about the ex–Afrika Korps driver. A solid frontline soldier. He glanced covertly at his escort: two Leibstandarte SS ghouls.

For the first time since receiving the order to report to GHQ, Berlin, Hellmann felt apprehensive. The encounter with the Feldgendarmerie seemed to have switched him back on. He no longer perceived the world through a mist. The world was suddenly very real, yet, paradoxically, utterly surreal. He was standing in the gardens of the New Chancellery, a few meters from the entrance to the Führerbunker itself. A mile away the Soviet artillery was still thundering. A dozen enlisted men were working in the garden, digging a wide trench. Whenever a Soviet shell exploded nearby they ducked their heads. Beyond the diggers stood a line of teen-age boys, all in the uniform of the Hitlerjugend. They were standing rigidly at attention, and they were flanked by two men. Hellmann recognized one of them from the newsreels. The receding hairline, the long nose, the liquid eyes. Artur Axmann, leader of the Hitlerjugend.

There was activity in the main entrance to the bunker and Hellmann noticed that his SS escorts stiffened. Figures were emerging from the bunker, like gray bears shambling out of a cave. The group moved slowly toward the line of Hitlerjugend. Suddenly Hellmann's throat went dry and his skin tingled.

In the center of the group was Adolf Hitler himself.

Hellmann's immediate reaction was blank disbelief. It was the Führer and yet it wasn't the Führer, *couldn't be* the Führer, that hunched, shuffling, palsied wreck of a man. Yet it was. There could be no mistaking those eyes, hot and ferocious, under the oversized visor of the cap. Or the simple uniform—pearl-gray tunic, green shirt, black trousers—even though the cloth was wrinkled and grubby and hung on the body in grotesque drapes and folds.

Hellmann had never been privileged to see Hitler in

the flesh. He knew him only from his portraits and from newsreels. The image he had of the Führer was the image projected by the Propaganda Ministry: the vibrant, tireless leader of the German people. He had heard rumors, of course—of illness, of only partial recovery from Stauffenberg's assassination attempt at Rastenburg. But nothing had prepared him for this caricature. It was revolting. Hitler was a stumbling corpse, the embodiment of the ruin he had brought upon his country and his people. Hellmann had often heard it muttered in messes and canteens in the Ardennes, and later in Holland, that Hitler was a suicidal madman with only one dream left: to drag the German Army, the German people, and the German state down with him in a Wagnerian climax of destruction. Well, here was the proof. It was terrifying to think that the destiny of the German Reich, such as it was, still lay in the hands of that twitching zombie.

Hellmann was suddenly afraid. Why had he been summoned? What did Bormann want of him?

Hitler was limping along the line of boys, pinning decorations on their tunics, saying a few words to each. Hellmann could not hear what he was saying. He could only observe the involuntary jerks and spasms in Hitler's arms and legs. But then he began to notice the reactions of the boys themselves. Their gray, pinched faces were radiant—with pride, admiration, unshakable devotion. Hitler's magnetism, that mysterious force that had once electrified the German people, had survived the disintegration of his body and his mind, and was still at work, still capable of firing the doomed with hope, the defeated with pride, the damned with some chimerical vision of salvation.

For the second time that day the image of Fuchs-

Jonesh invaded Hellmann's mind. He remembered that for all Hitler's ranting grossness, his inhuman isolation, his cruelty, he had rid Germany of the Fuchs-Joneshes. Hitler had offered real hope, real pride, real salvation in exchange for the bankruptcy and humiliation of the Republic. And he had taken a terrible revenge on the Fuchs-Joneshes. Hellmann could recall vividly his own feeling of exultation at the bombing of London, at the seemingly endless victories of the Germans over the British. The triumph had been short-lived, yes. The British and their allies were now dismembering Germany. But one could not forget the early years. Germany restored. Germany triumphant. German shame wiped out. One *should* not forget.

The Hitlerjugend were marching away and Hitler and his aides were vanishing back inside the bunker. There was a spring in the boys' steps. Hellmann sensed that they would let themselves be crushed under the treads of the Soviet tanks before surrendering an inch of ground.

One of his escort touched him on the arm. He moved forward, between the two SS men, toward the bunker. *One should not forget.* Half of him insisted on that. Yet the other half told him that it had all been a monstrous fraud, that Hitler and his henchmen were a bunch of gangsters who had manipulated events for short-term gain and had then led the German people toward the greatest humiliation in their long history.

Divided in himself, Hellmann entered the bunker. His stomach turned over. The stench of sour sweat, cigarette smoke, rotting cabbage, and latrines was suffocating. The ventilation system collected odors from every corner of the underground complex, mixed them together, and distributed them through the rooms and corridors. Hellmann remembered a hut in Norway in which he and his unit had been holed up for two weeks during blizzards—how two of his men had gone mad through claustrophobia, how others had rapidly abandoned any attempt to keep themselves clean. They had simply festered.

He was astonished by the Lilliputian scale of the bunker. The command center of the Third Reich had been compressed into a rat-run of tiny whitewashed rooms and passages built as a makeshift air-raid shelter. Bottles and papers littered the floor of the main corridor. The fetid air vibrated with the clacking of typewriters and teleprinters. Naked light bulbs lit corridors thronged with officers, SS guards, chauffeurs, couriers, and members of Hitler's personal staff.

Hellmann and his escort halted at a steel door guarded by four Leibstandarte troopers. Hellmann was checked and searched and then ushered into a long, narrow room, a continuation of the main corridor, whose walls were covered with military maps. At least a dozen different conversations were in progress, ranging in volume from whispers to shouts. Hellmann caught a glimpse of Hitler leaning over a map of Berlin with generals Krebs and Burgdorf. By the table stood Bormann and Speer, Minister of Armaments and Munitions. There were also several Gauleiters from Berlin and its suburbs, some adjutants, two female secretaries, and Hitler's chauffeur-bodyguard, Erich Kempka. Nobody took any notice of Hellmann. He stood at attention between his SS escorts and waited, feeling at once trapped and fascinated. The tumult of voices diminished somewhat and he was able to distinguish Hitler's harsh tones.

"Can we still count on good radio contact?"

"Yes, my Führer," General Krebs replied. "The Signal Corps has put up an antennae-carrying balloon and we're receiving information about conditions at the front."

"Good. I want clear, concise answers on five points. Make a note of this, Krebs. Where are Wenck's forward positions? When is he going to resume his attack? Where is the Ninth Army? When does it expect to make its breakthrough? And where are Holste's forward positions? Do you have all that?"

"Yes, my Führer."

"What is Dr. Goebbels up to?" Hitler asked suddenly, on a tangent, not addressing anyone in particular.

"He is meeting with his assistants." It was a woman's voice, one of Hitler's secretaries, a pretty, blond girl, Gerda Christian. "He's in conference but he should be here any minute."

"I want to see him as soon as he gets here."

Hellmann noticed that Gerda Christian's movements were jerky, almost a parody of Hitler's. He examined the other faces. A nervous tic in General Krebs's cheek made him look as if he were permanently winking. Burgdorf had the air of a man with a massive hangover. He kept clearing his throat, as though about to make a speech. But he was silent. Hellmann could sense unbearable tensions, fears, and mutual hatreds just below the surface. These people were entombed without any possibility of escape—and they knew it.

"Captain Hellmann?"

A soft, pleasant voice.

Hellmann turned.

Bormann.

The all-powerful Minister was smiling faintly. In complete contrast to the others he looked relaxed, in his element. Hellmann saluted and concentrated on making his own face expressionless. It was safer that way.

"Come with me, please, Captain."

Bormann led him across the room toward a door bearing a gilded eagle. Hellmann suddenly noticed that Hitler had left the conference room, that the door he was approaching must lead into the Führer's office, that he was about to come face-to-face with Adolf Hitler. He physically braced himself as Bormann tapped on the door and opened it. He followed Bormann inside.

Hitler was seated stiffly at a desk, under a portrait of Frederick the Great. He appeared to be tapping with his hand on the surface of the desk, but Hellmann realized that the movement was involuntary, a muscular spasm. Hitler's head was sunk deep between his rounded shoulders. On his left breast he wore his golden Party badge and the Iron Cross he had won in the First World War. There were stains of tea and food on his jacket.

"My Führer," Bormann said, "may I present Captain Hellmann, holder of the Iron Cross First Class. He has come from Magdeburg at your special order."

Hitler looked up. His eyes were a pale gray-blue, opaque, bloodshot. The legendary Hitler eyes. A pair of peeled grapes! And below them, purplish sacks of sagging skin. His whole face was a slack, expressionless mask of yellowish tissue—but no, not quite expressionless. The lips were moving, to form the mirthless approximation of a smile.

"Good," Hitler said. "Good. It is fortunate that there are still devoted soldiers courageously serving their Führer and the Reich. I am surrounded by traitors and

17

spies." His voice trailed away. And then he suddenly barked: "Cowards!"

Hellmann allowed himself to relax very slightly. There was nothing so formidable about Hitler after all. One could almost pity him. He clicked his heels and bowed.

"Have you any idea why you've been brought here, Captain?" Bormann asked with a friendly smile.

"No, Herr Minister."

"You are fluent in English, I believe? Also, you have expert knowledge of British and American military practices. So you possess all the qualifications for the successful completion of a certain mission."

Hellmann said nothing. Bormann was holding up a sheet of flimsy paper.

"Listen to this," Bormann went on. "It is a statement issued by Reichsmarschall Hermann Göring: *'My Führer, since you have decided to remain at your post in the besieged fortress of Berlin, do you agree that I take over at once the total leadership of the Reich with full freedom of action at home and abroad, in accordance with your decree of June 29, 1941? If no reply is received by ten o'clock tonight I shall take it for granted that you have lost your freedom of action, and shall assume that the conditions required for the implementation of the law have been met.'"*

"What do you think of this?"

Hellmann started. He couldn't help himself. Hitler's sudden hoarse blare after Bormann's soft tones was like an explosion.

"You . . . Captain. What do you think? As a loyal soldier."

Hellmann stared at Hitler. There was a light in the famous eyes now, a mesmeric glare that matched the hysteria in the voice. Still, it was easy enough to find a reply: the question implied its own answer.

"I think it is treason, my Führer."

"You are right, Captain. It is treason. Hermann Göring is a criminal, an outlaw. He is under arrest."

For a moment Hellmann failed to grasp the staggering significance of Hitler's statement.

"The former Reichsmarschall was arrested by a detachment of SS," Bormann was saying. "He will be taken from Obersalzberg to Mauterndorf today."

Hellmann just looked at him. It was astounding. King Hermann fallen. No more fanfares, no more palaces, no more beautiful mistresses, ornate uniforms . . .

"Officially," Bormann went on, "the Reichsmarschall has resigned his post for reasons of health. It is the Führer's legitimate desire, however, to ensure that the traitor pays the price for his treason."

Hellmann glanced at Hitler. There was a plate of cakes on the desk. Hitler was playing with the crumbs, sullen and introspective.

Hellmann tried to think. Obviously fat Hermann was to be killed. But what the hell did it have to do with him? Bormann seemed to read his mind.

"The Führer has sentenced Göring to death," he said quietly. "It is not only a question of justice, but also of policy. Göring has betrayed us once and is no doubt ready to do so again—by handing himself over to the British or the Americans, for example. Therefore his execution is a matter of urgent necessity."

Hellmann cleared his throat and chose his words carefully. "I understand, Minister. But surely if he has already been arrested . . . ?" He allowed his voice to trail away.

Bormann smiled thinly.

"You may be forgiven for assuming that in the hands of the SS Göring's fate is sealed. As a loyal, frontline soldier you would not appreciate the"—he hesitated for a second—"political situation. The fact is, Captain, that there are certain elements, even among the SS, who cannot be trusted."

Hellmann knew enough about the rivalries among Hitler's senior courtiers to appreciate the significance of Bormann's hesitation before the word "political." A subtle but direct attack on Heinrich Himmler. Clearly, the arch-schemer Bormann was behind the death sentence on Göring. Was Himmler to be his next target?

"Our Führer," Bormann added, "has only the most limited confidence in the people holding Göring."

"I am surrounded by traitors and spies."

Again, Hellmann started at the sudden eruption of Hitler's voice. He realized, too, that the Führer's ranting against traitors and spies was a kind of litany, a litany fostered by Bormann, and the key to the Minister's power. Clearly Bormann intended to use Hitler's obsession with spies and traitors to eliminate all his rivals. What Hellmann could not fathom was *why*. With Germany collapsing round him, with total defeat only days away, what in God's name was the point in Bormann playing out his deadly game?

"Your assignment, Captain," Bormann said, "is to make absolutely certain that the Führer's orders are carried out. You will take the former Reichsmarschall into custody and personally supervise his liquidation."

For a second Hellmann examined the possibility of following his natural inclination and refusing the mission. But no. If he did that, he would never leave the bunker alive. He would be instantly categorized as a traitor and a spy and summarily shot. So he snapped to attention and nodded his head crisply, calculating that even if he was able to leave besieged Berlin, by the time he reached Bavaria the war would probably be over and Göring either a prisoner of the Allies or dead by his own hand.

He turned to Bormann. "What means would I have at my disposal for this mission? What authority would I be granted?" It was impossible to sound enthusiastic but at least he could appear to be soldierly.

Hitler answered him.

"Your authority will be unlimited."

Hitler rose. Supporting himself on the massive walnut desk he shuffled toward Hellmann, like a very old man in carpet slippers.

"As to the means at your disposal: a Fieseler Storch is waiting to fly you out of Berlin. You will proceed to Brno in Czechoslovakia where some old acquaintances are expecting your arrival. I'm referring to our mercenaries of the Britisches Freikorps of the SS. We have no fears about their loyalty."

"Precisely," Bormann said. "They have no choice but to remain loyal. They are concerned only with saving their own necks. They will assist you in capturing Göring from his guards and they will execute him without remorse. In exchange they will receive new identity papers and a sizable cash bonus."

Hellmann tried to keep the dismay out of his face. He had assumed that the Britisches Freikorps, the unit he had trained a year ago, had been disbanded. He had loathed every minute of that posting, loathed every single one of the men he had been ordered to train. If it was assassins Hitler and Bormann wanted they couldn't have chosen more wisely: the Britisches Freikorps was a refuge for pathological killers, fanatics, and degenerates. By the same token, it looked as if this mission was serious. He had assumed that once safely out of Berlin he could vanish discreetly in the general confusion but . . .

"One final detail," Bormann said. He was smiling, and again Hellmann had the uncomfortable feeling that the Minister was reading his mind. "I have appointed an officer to assist you in your mission. Lieutenant Wrack is a frontline soldier like yourself. If anything . . . untoward were to happen to you, Lieutenant Wrack would take over command."

The threat was perfectly plain: one wrong move and you will be terminated.

Bormann picked up a thick folder and handed it to Hellmann. "This contains the individual dossiers on the members of the Britisches Freikorps who will participate in the mission."

Hellmann took the folder.

"I understand that you may feel that the operation has a distasteful side, Captain," Bormann said, more gently. "But remember that you will be executing a traitor under orders—orders you have received from the lips of the Führer himself. In the circumstances, it's a challenge. It won't be easy. You are an officer of exceptional ability. General Göhler himself has vouched for your loyalty. That is why you have been chosen."

There was nothing Hellmann could do but salute.

Hitler spoke, a dribble of saliva hanging from a corner of his mouth.

"The final outcome of the war will be decided here, in Berlin," he said. "All is not lost. The Russians will suffer the greatest defeat, the bloodiest defeat of their history at the gates of this city. Remember Frederick the Great in 1762. It is only treachery and faintheartedness that can prevent me from dealing the Bolshevik colossus the fatal blow. The Red Army will bleed to death in the battle for Berlin. General Wenck's army is moving up from the south. He will drive the Russians back."

He was panting. He swayed against the desk, then recovered sufficiently to add in a voice that carried a distant echo of the mass rallies of his heyday: "Hermann Göring has sold himself to the Bolsheviks and the Jews."

Hellmann glanced covertly at Bormann. He was nodding his agreement. But could he possibly believe a single word of Hitler's fantasy of destroying the Red Army at the gates of Berlin? Did Hitler himself believe it?

"That will be all for the moment, Captain," Bormann said.

Hellmann saluted again, and turned to Hitler, assuming that the Führer would have a parting message for him. But Hitler had turned his back. He was limping slowly and painfully toward his chair. He stopped, staring up at the portrait of Frederick the Great. He seemed mesmerized by it. Seconds passed in silence. Then Bormann gestured curtly for Hellmann to leave. Hellmann saluted once more, turned, and walked briskly to the door.

5

"Well, my Führer?" Bormann leaned over the desk. Hitler was in his chair, again toying with crumbs of cake. "What is your impression of Captain Hellmann? Do you think he'll do?"

A moment went by and only the rumbling of the heavy artillery broke the silence. Finally, Hitler looked up.

"I think he can do it. The only question is his loyalty. How much of a hold do we have on the man?"

Bormann hesitated, then answered: "He isn't married. His father is deceased and his mother was reported missing, but fortunately, he has one younger sister. I think we have quite a good hold on our Captain Hellmann."

Hitler nodded, then remained motionless for several minutes. Bormann was about to leave, assuming that Hitler had relapsed into one of his dozes. But just as his hand closed on the doorknob, Hitler's voice barked out: "You've given this mission the code name Fenris . . .?"

"It refers to a figure from Scandinavian mythology," Bormann replied a little hesitantly; Hitler considered himself an expert on Nordic myth. "You remember, my Führer, in Asgard's *The Twilight of the Gods*, Fenris was the name of Thor's wolf. His jaws could crush his master's enemies. I thought the name appropriate."

Hitler's face twitched.

"Yes," he said. "The twilight of the gods." He smiled slackly. "Good."

Bormann closed the door behind him. Operation Fenris was well and truly launched. Now there was only Himmler to deal with. *Der treue Heinrich.*

APRIL 27, 1945, 5:00 P.M.

"This whole business is grotesque," Hermann Göring whined as he sank back onto the vast canopied bed, which shuddered under his weight. "Sooner or later the Führer will see his mistake and put me in charge of the negotiations."

Turning to the manservant who stood impassively by the bed, Göring tossed him his tunic, heavy with decorations and epaulettes, then reread the message that the SS Kommandant in the next room had transmitted to him.

"Effective immediately, Hermann Göring is removed from all functions, and is no longer in line for succession to the supreme office. You are to place him under immediate arrest for the crime of high treason. If the Führer has died you are to liquidate the traitor immediately."

"Grotesque," Göring repeated. "Absurd. Completely absurd. The Führer can't have decreed any such idiocy. What do you make of it, Emil?"

The manservant was concerned less about his master's fate than the stationing of an SS detachment at the castle. But he nodded gravely in an apparent gesture of agreement. He gave the tunic an energetic brushing and placed it on a hanger in the closet. Then he went over to the chest of drawers, on which stood a large bottle of codeine pills.

"Under arrest!" Göring muttered. "It's that madman Bormann. Taking advantage of the Führer's momentary depression. You know, Emil, they all hate me. All of them—Bormann, Himmler, Speer, and von Ribbentrop. They all want my post. They want to steal what I have earned by a lifetime of devotion to the cause of National Socialism."

He sighed heavily as Emil unscrewed the cap of the bottle. But before the manservant could hand him the pills the door was flung open and a harsh, high-pitched voice shouted: "Drop that!"

Emil was so startled that he literally dropped the bottle. Pills cascaded onto the floor. The owner of the high-pitched voice, a wiry SS officer, with a prominent Adam's apple, advanced toward the bed. With slow deliberation he systematically crushed the spilt pills to powder with the heel of his boot.

"I protest," Göring said, but with little conviction. "There are certain rights due to my rank and I intend to have them respected. I am under medical care. The tablets are part of my daily regime."

The officer ignored him. He snapped his fingers at Emil. The servant obediently stooped and retrieved the bottle, in which a few pills remained. He handed the bottle to the officer. Without another word the SS man stalked out of the room.

Göring lay on the bed, his face puckered, like a huge baby about to bawl. After a moment, he struggled into a sitting position.

"Emil"—it was almost a whimper—"do we have a reserve supply?"

Emil shook his head.

"I want to see my wife. Fetch her up. And Emil—you must obtain some more of my tablets. I'll pay anything. Anything."

Emil avoided his master's eye.

"I'll do my best," he muttered. He had never understood Göring's dependence on the codeine pills. But there was no doubt that the Reichsmarschall was addicted. The trouble was, he doubted Göring's ability to pay. As he left the room, his mind was totally occupied with plans to save his own skin. Hermann Göring was a sinking ship, that was plain.

7

Hellmann blew on the stub of his cigarette and lit a fresh one from the glowing end. Since his audience with Hitler and some desultory conversation with SS guards, he had done nothing but chain-smoke and think. He was alone in a small, square, whitewashed room, sparsely furnished as an office. On the other side of the door, he knew, were two Leibstandarte guards. He was trapped—in every sense of the word. Trapped in the bunker, trapped in the insane mission dreamed up by a pathological killer and his henchman, for that was what Hitler and Bormann were, he had decided.

The door opened and Bormann stepped into the room. Hellmann rose. Bormann wrinkled his nose: the air was thick with cigarette smoke.

"Please refrain from smoking. The Führer may appear at any moment and he detests tobacco."

Hellmann stubbed out his cigarette.

"Sit down, Captain. I have a few questions to ask you."

Bormann hitched a thigh onto a corner of the desk.

"According to your file, you were born in 1915. So you are now thirty?"

"Nearly."

"But still single?"

Hellmann was puzzled by this line of questioning. What the hell did his love life have to do with anything?

"I haven't met the right woman yet." He made himself smile and added: "In the last few years I haven't had much opportunity to meet the right woman."

Bormann matched Hellmann's smile.

"I understand that," he said. "So. You would say that you had no . . . shall we call them . . . emotional attachments."

Hellmann shook his head.

"You find my questions strange," Bormann went on. "But it is my experience that the type of mission for which you have been selected is better suited to a man with no romantic ties. I have known so many operations to fail because officers were more concerned with the well-being of their families than with their work. I am delighted that this does not apply to you." Bormann smiled again. "Your record in Crete and Norway is exemplary. And you performed splendidly in Operation Dragon, during the Ardennes counteroffensive. But—and there's always a but—the mission that our Führer has entrusted to you won't be like anything you've handled up to now. And I thought I sensed a certain degree of . . . reluctance when you were told of your objective."

So, Hellmann thought, he did read my mind.

"I have to admit I was taken aback for a moment," Hellmann said. "But I assure you, Herr Minister, that it was only for a moment."

"Very natural. You were no doubt a little uneasy about being ordered to Berlin. And then coming face-to-face with our supreme leader. But, of course, you are delighted at having this opportunity to serve the Führer directly."

Hellmann couldn't work out whether Bormann was subtly mocking him or whether he really believed what he was saying. But the Minister's next statement was unequivocal enough.

"The Führer places his entire confidence in you, Captain, and I hope, for your sake, that his trust is merited. The Führer wants the matter of Hermann Göring closed. Rapidly and completely. Do I make myself clear?"

"Perfectly clear, Herr Minister."

"Good. You will find detailed instructions in the file I gave you. And Lieutenant Wrack will give you a complete briefing."

Bormann rose and Hellmann rose with him. Bormann opened the door and the two SS guards snapped to attention. Colonel Högl, head of Hitler's bodyguard, was standing in the passageway.

"Högl, you will escort Captain Hellmann," Bormann said.

Then he turned to Hellmann. He was smiling again. "Good-bye, Captain Hellmann. And good hunting." He paused deliberately, then added: "Remember, the Führer's eyes are on you."

Hellmann followed Högl up the main staircase and along the wide corridor that was the communal dining room of the bunker. People were drinking and smoking. Hellmann lit up, gratefully inhaling a deep lungful of smoke. Högl turned left, toward the double steel doors that led into the garden of the Foreign Ministry.

There was a slight delay as Högl showed his pass to the guards, then Hellmann was out, out into the bitter cold of the Berlin dusk that seemed as fresh and clean as white wine after the tomblike atmosphere of the bunker.

But as he marched briskly beside Högl he knew that he had escaped the bunker only in the most superficial sense. Bormann's parting shot guaranteed that.

"Remember, the Führer's eyes are on you."

8

The runway was an alarmingly short-looking stretch of the East-West Axis road, cleared of rubble by a Volkssturm company.

The pilot of the two-seater Fieseler Storch was a young Luftwaffe tearaway who smoked long, thin Russian cigarettes and who affected an air of devil-may-care recklessness.

Hellmann experienced a moment of pure terror as the plane took off in the light of the artillery flashes and struggled for height in a hail of bullets.

To steady himself Hellmann yelled, "Flak?" above the howl of the engine.

The pilot shook his head, grinning.

"Small arms. Peashooters. Relax."

But Hellmann was thinking about Reichsmarschall von Greim and Hanna Reitsch, who had flown into Berlin the day before. The bunker had been buzzing with the story of their dramatic, heroic arrival. But the fact was that von Greim had been badly wounded in the foot. The reflection that his mission might well end suddenly and bloodily before it had even begun gave Hellmann an intense desire to live.

As they flew low over Grünewald and the Havel River, Hellmann made himself a promise: he would survive, at all costs.

After what seemed like only moments they landed at Berlin's Gatow Airport, which was under heavy bombardment.

The inevitable SS officers emerged from the dark to escort him to an old, ungainly Ju-52 transport aircraft.

A man was standing by the plane, a tall, thin man whose eyes were gray and cold under the peak of his cap. He saluted smartly.

"Lieutenant Wrack."

Hellmann acknowledged the salute and climbed into the plane after Wrack. There were two folding bunks in the aft section. Hellmann lay down and prepared himself for another nerve-tearing takeoff, pulling the hood of his coat round his head, deliberately avoiding Wrack's eye.

He closed his eyes as the old Junker's engines wheezed into life. After a series of sickening bumps and lurches, the aircraft clawed aloft and gradually stabilized.

The curtains dividing the cockpit from the aft section parted and the co-pilot emerged in search of a match.

"What about enemy fighters?" Hellmann asked him.

The co-pilot shrugged, bracing himself against the fuselage as the plane hit turbulence. "No problem. It's night. Ivan needs everything he's got for Berlin. Relax," he added as he turned to make his way back to the cockpit.

The repetition of the advice to relax, the whole crazy situation, suddenly struck Hellmann as absurdly comic. He began to shake with laughter. He was aware of Wrack's icy gaze on him.

"Something amuses you, Captain?" Wrack said.

Hellmann turned to meet that gray, level stare.

"Yes," he said.

"May I share the joke?"

After a moment, Hellmann said: "I don't know you of course, Lieutenant, but something tells me that you wouldn't get the joke."

Hellmann noticed the silver insignia on the collar tabs of Wrack's tunic.

"SS," he said.

"Yes."

"And where were you serving before this mission?"

"In Berlin. I was placed on special orders from HQ last December. Is there anything else I can tell you?"

Hellmann smiled. "Not for the moment. We'll get to know each other."

He flipped on a small light over his bunk and opened the folder Bormann had given him.

"Before you brief me, I want to look through this."

The first documents in the folder were the personal files on five members of the the Britisches Freikorps. Hellmann winced at the names: Ward, O'Mara, Chandra, Legge, Duval. God, what a collection.

And on top of them, Lieutenant Wrack. Bormann's creature. He could feel Wrack's eyes still on him.

Hellmann switched off the light and settled down to sleep. He was going to survive, but it was going to take everything he knew.

9

Wrack's voice dragged Hellmann out of a deep, dreamless sleep, the first real sleep he had enjoyed for weeks.

"Wake up, Captain. We'll be landing in ten minutes."

"What's the time?" Hellmann mumbled. His mouth tasted sour. He struggled into a sitting position.

"Just after twenty hundred."

Hellmann grunted and fumbled for a cigarette. He saw that Wrack was holding Bormann's folder.

"Tell me about these Britisches Freikorps men," Wrack said. "You've worked with them before?"

"Haven't you read my file?"

Wrack shrugged, unabashed. "I would like your personal impression of them."

"I helped train them. I was never on active service with them." He smiled. Wrack was an easy man to mock and he certainly deserved mockery. "The Führer thinks they're the right men for this mission. Are you going to argue with the Führer?"

Wrack ignored this.

"Tell me about Ward," he said.

"Why Ward in particular?"

"He's the senior officer."

"You've got the file."

"What do you personally think of Ward?"

"What the hell does it matter what I think?"

Hellmann laughed shortly. "If you want to know, I think that Ward, Thomas William, is the nearest thing to a piece of shit that a human being can be."

"He appears to be a most capable soldier—according to his file."

"Certainly. But then a file doesn't tell you everything."

"What should I know about Ward?"

Hellmann decided to tell him. Why not?

"Ward led a Commando expedition in the Lofoten Islands in 1943. He was captured, along with ten of his men. They all got the death sentence. But Ward happened to have an old friend who was working in the Abwehr. You've probably heard of him. Von Hagen."

"Von Hagen. Yes. He lost an arm fighting the Czech partisans. An aristocrat." He loaded the word with contempt.

"Yes. And so is Ward—or at least he was a rich man—a Junker in Northern Ireland. Before the war he was a playboy. He met von Hagen in Vienna. They were both finalists in some smart fencing tournament."

"And von Hagen saved his friend's life? That's interesting."

"On condition that he joined the Britisches Freikorps. His men, incidentally, were all shot."

There was the ghost of a smile on Wrack's hard face. "And you consider that was conduct unbecoming to an officer and a gentleman?" The sarcasm was obvious.

"I consider it conduct unbecoming to anyone."

Wrack smiled, more broadly this time.

"But after all, Captain," he said, "he was only trying

to survive. One could forgive him for that."

"One could. But the point about Ward is that he cannot forgive himself. Self-hatred, Lieutenant Wrack, can turn a man into a very dangerous beast."

"Precisely the sort of man required for this operation. In any case, if you'll permit me to say so, your theories about Ward seem rather extravagant to me."

"You asked."

The plane was losing height rapidly. The co-pilot poked his head through the curtains and indicated, with a gesture, that they were going in to land.

They hit the runway hard, bounced twice, and rolled to a halt with every rivet in the rusty fuselage shrieking.

Blue lights winked on and off and the pilot emerged from the cockpit pulling on a very battered U.S. Air Corps flying jacket.

"Nasty weather, Captain," he said. "I had a job, I'll tell you."

He unbolted the fuselage door and leaned out. A small blizzard of snow, whipped by a chill wind, blew into the aircraft.

"You can disembark," the pilot said. "Your reception committee is waiting."

Hellmann jumped down to the concrete runway; Wrack followed. The beams of several flashlights wavered in the darkness. Seconds later, a field car escorted by two motorcyclists astride huge BMW machines rolled to a halt under the starboard wing. In the double beam of the car's headlights a young, square-jawed officer appeared. His sleeve bore the emblem of Das Reich Division of the SS.

"Captain Vögler," he said, with a salute. "Field Marschall Schörner has asked me to look after you."

Wrack and Hellmann climbed into the backseat of the car. It made a wide circle, then accelerated down the runway, flanked by the two outriders. At the main gate of the airfield, the little convoy stopped and an MP examined the passengers in the beam of his flashlight. He saluted and the barrier rose. As the car gathered speed Vögler asked conversationally: "How are things in Berlin?"

Wrack said nothing. After a moment Hellmann said, diplomatically: "The situation is . . . difficult. What about here?"

"Not too bad . . . at the moment. Last we heard, the Americans were a hundred to a hundred and fifty kilometers away at most. The Russians haven't turned up yet. There are a few partisan groups—in reality nothing but bands of deserters." A hint of awe crept into his voice. "I believe you have seen the Führer?"

"Yes," Hellmann replied neutrally.

"I've only seen him once." Vögler was almost gushing. "At Heydrich's funeral in '42. But he made an unforgettable impression on me. You have actually spoken to him. I envy you, Captain."

For a moment Vögler sounded uncannily like Hellmann's father. The old language teacher had venerated Hitler and had even been presented to him, a year or two before the war, at some Party occasion. He had been an enthusiastic Party member, regarding Hitler, rightly it seemed at the time, as the savior of the lower middle class. His mother, on the other hand, had objected violently to Hitler and the Nazis from the start, not on any ideological grounds—the Party's anti-Jewish platform rather appealed to her—but out of snobbery. As a cousin, several times removed, of a ruined member of the minor

Bavarian nobility, she considered it outrageous that a jumped-up Austrian corporal could rule Germany.

"It must have been an extraordinary experience," Vögler was saying.

"It was," Hellmann replied, with absolute truth. He decided to change the subject. "Have our men arrived?"

"There's been a delay," Vögler said as the car passed the first houses in the old Czech town. "But the convoy bringing them here should arrive within the next hour or two."

Hellmann nodded and fished through his pockets for a cigarette. Vögler turned round on his seat and struck a match for him.

"Your mission is really vital, isn't it, Captain?"

"It is," Hellmann said, with a quick glance at Wrack. "I gather Berlin hasn't filled you in on the details?"

"Not at all."

The snow had now changed to icy rain. The car crossed a narrow steel bridge and entered a little square dominated by a grandiose equestrian statue.

The Kommandantur of Brno was located in what had been the town's main hotel. But the local Wehrmacht garrison had transformed the building into a fortress. The entrance appeared to be blocked from every angle by walls of sandbags studded with machine-gun slits. In fact, there was a passageway wide enough to accommodate the car and its motorcycle escorts.

The inner courtyard, with its moss-grown fountain, was jammed with scout cars, armored cars, and tanks. Opel trucks stood next to heavily armored Pumas. Beside two tracked vehicles was a huge Jagdpanther with its turreted 88 mm gun. Soldiers were lugging drums of petrol past these machines, while others staggered under the weight of ammunition cases. Volleys of shouts and curses rang out in the chill night air.

The field car and its outriders pulled up near a group of signal corpsmen busily preparing field telephones. Briskly, Captain Vögler climbed the stairs leading to the entrance of the Kommandantur. Wrack and Hellmann followed. They crossed a lobby cluttered with cases, heaps of files, and cloth-covered typewriters, and entered a room furnished with a long table and half a dozen chairs. The walls still bore the marks of tapestries and paintings hastily removed.

"You're packing up?" Hellmann asked, as Vögler waved them to a table loaded with mettwurst, ersatz bread, and bottles of wine and beer.

"Not yet. But we expect to pull back to Prague. Orders."

Hellmann opened a bottle of beer and helped himself hungrily to the mettwurst.

"Just between us," Vögler said confidentially, "it's the first time I've ever heard of a British volunteer SS corps. Field Marschall Schörner didn't seem to know any more about them than I did. When he received the call from Berlin, it took him two hours to locate the unit. Can you beat that? In his own army group!"

"How many of them do we have?"

"About thirty. From what I hear, there were about forty-five of them last year, plus another hundred that the Ministry of Propaganda used for statements over the radio and in press articles. In December they were assigned to a battalion in the Death's-Head Division on the Oder Front. By January some of them were proving so unruly that the unit had to be disbanded. The survivors were sent to a camp outside Prague. That's where your five were selected when the directive came in from Berlin. One of them's an Anglo-Indian or something. How the hell did he end up in the SS?"

Hellmann took a long pull of his beer. He decided he rather liked Vögler.

"Anglo-Indian Waffen SS outfits were set up after Rommel's victories in 1941 and 1942," he said. "We bagged more than one hundred and fifty thousand prisoners of war in Libya and Tunisia. In 1941 the Führer met Subhas Chandra Bose, the Indian nationalist leader. Bose furnished the cadre for an Indian National Army but it never really existed, except on paper. It was made up of about two thousand men recruited from North African POW camps. They were garrisoned in a quiet sector—the south of France, near the Pyrenees. Then they were moved to Germany in July 1944, leaving behind most of their equipment. Right now, the Indians are just outside Berlin."

"What about the English? How did we get them into the SS?"

"Berger organized a recruitment campaign in the POW camps with the help of John Amery, the son of Churchill's Secretary of State for India. The project was a failure, except from the propaganda standpoint. At first, the volunteers were known as the British Legion of St. George. Later on they became the British Free Corps. Their enlistment contract stipulated that they would fight only on the Eastern Front as part of the anti-Bolshevik crusade."

Hellmann took another bottle of beer and stretched his legs under the table. Outside, the icy rain drove against the windows. The snug warmth of the room was making him drowsy. The door opened, and an orderly appeared.

"The men you have been expecting are here, Captain. There's a Czech with them," he added.

"Bring me the Czech and put the rest in another office."

When the orderly had left, Wrack asked: "What's this about a Czech? We weren't told about him."

"He's from the USB," Vögler replied. "Ustredna Statnej Bezpecnostic. The political police of the Independent Slovakian State. He'll be your guide for the first hundred kilometers. He'll make sure that you don't stumble into any skirmishes with the armed bands operating in the southern part of the province."

"Can we trust him?"

"Well, a price has been placed on his head by the Czech resistance and the government-in-exile in London, so he should be loyal. But watch him just the same. You can pick up your men as soon as we work out the details of your departure."

"What about transport vehicles?" Hellmann asked. "We're going to need something fast, maneuverable—a Horch, for example."

"That's a possibility."

"And extra petrol for the trip."

"That's no problem."

The door swung open again and a thickset man with a square face walked in. He was wearing a leather military coat and his felt boots tracked mud across the parquet floor. He strode up to the table and, without ceremony, helped himself to a beer, which he drank at a gulp, then wiped his mouth with the back of his sleeve.

"You must be Hellmann and you—you must be Wrack," said the Czech in heavily accented German.

"And you—who are you?" Wrack asked glacially.

"You can call me Stachek."

10

Ward stood by a window, staring out at the courtyard of the Kommandantur, where gusts of wind were whipping the rain into spirals. The old Etonian former Commando officer wore a standard German Army uniform, with SS insignia. On the sleeves of his tunic, below the badge denoting his rank of captain, was a Union Jack and the letters BFC. His dark brown hair was short and brushed straight back from his forehead. His eyes, set close together above a high-bridged nose, were as black as olives. Except for the chin, which receded into the neck, it was a strong face, set into a permanent expression of scorn.

On the far side of the room O'Mara was holding forth. His voice, with its Irish brogue, was raised—deliberately. He was, as usual, reminiscing about his days in the IRA in the hope of goading Ward, whom he saw as the embodiment of the Protestant Ascendancy, and whom he hated accordingly.

"Explosives are like women, old Murphy used to tell us lads," O'Mara was saying. "You've got to treat them gentle. Don't rush them. Handle them right and you'll get what you want from them."

Duval, the French Canadian, who was the only one

listening, smiled out of politeness. Duval was always polite.

"I can hear him now," O'Mara went on. "Little old man he was, like a yard of thread—but Jesus he was a hard bastard. He taught me how to blow up a mess hall full of Brits with a ten-inch piece of copper tube and a pack of playing cards."

Duval was interested but skeptical. "Playing cards?"

"Isn't that right now, Captain?" O'Mara appealed to Ward, in the hope of some reaction. He was disappointed. Ward merely shrugged.

"I have no idea," he said.

"Playing cards," Duval repeated. "You joke with me."

"It's no joke when it goes off in a Belfast pub on a Saturday night. Your ordinary pack of washable cards contains a little something called nitrocellulose. Under high pressure it's an explosive. So what you do is cut up the cards. Then you plug one end of your tube with copper solder and pack in the shredded cards. Protestant confetti, we used to call it. Your detonator is nothing but a few match heads. You put them in with the confetti and seal the end. Then you stroll into a pub, drop the little beauty into the fire, and stroll out. The heat and pressure reach the critical point and"—he flung up his arms— "you watch them peel pieces of British soldiers off the walls from the corner of the street."

"Is it true that the Irish Republican Army shoots its pederasts?"

Legge's languid drawl trickled across the room from the sagging horsehair sofa in the corner, on which he was lying with his eyes closed.

O'Mara grinned.

"Put it this way," he said, "I wouldn't advise *you* to sign up, now."

"Fortunately," Legge said, "I have never been physically attracted by the Irish. Not even by a sensitive young poet."

There was silence. Legge's remarks, cryptic or outrageous, and delivered in an exaggerated upper-class accent, often had that effect.

Chandra, the fifth man, was pacing up and down. He was young, in his early twenties. His head was shaved to a dark stubble, and in the tawny color and smooth texture of his skin it was clear that his father's Indian genes had predominated over those of his English mother.

This was a fact that Chandra had found it prudent to conceal from Standartenführer Dr. Scheffer, of the Ahnenerbe Institute for Research into Heredity—patron: Heinrich Himmler. Scheffer had interviewed him in the POW camp nine months after he had been captured in the fall of Tobruk. Naturally plausible, quick-witted, and charming, Chandra had told Dr. Scheffer what Dr. Scheffer was desperately anxious to hear: that he was a Tibetan of purebred Indo-Aryan stock. Within weeks Chandra found himself accompanying Scheffer on a bizarre, top-secret research expedition to Tibet, or the "cradle of the Indo-Aryan race," as the balding, bespectacled little Herr Doktor called it. And then that castle, lost in the empty forests of Bavaria, Schloss Adler. Scheffer in a gray suit a size too large for him, garrulous with nerves. Vast stone corridors lined with statues in niches, the heroes of Nazi mythology: Henry the Fowler, Henry the Lion, Albrecht the Bear, Frederick Barbarossa, Frederick the Great, and, of course, Adolf Hitler. Then a vast, echoing hall with a vaulted ceiling and Himmler himself sitting at the head of a refectory table. The Mongoloid face. The bloodless slit of a mouth. Eyes of terrifying coldness behind thick glasses. Chandra had quailed. Bamboozling a harmless little German crank was one thing; trying to pull the wool over Heinrich Himmler's shark's eyes was another. But Himmler had exhibited him to the assembled company with pride, enthusing over his "quill-thin nose," prominent jaw, deep-set eyes, and "facial symmetry."

"Chandra, dear"—Legge's voice was theatrically plaintive—"*would* you stop doing a Felix? My nerve ends are twanging like an ill-tuned fiddle."

Chandra obligingly stopped pacing and Legge closed his eyes again with a sigh, stretching. For all his affected speech and mannerisms Legge was a large, powerfully built man. He had the face of a degenerate cherub. When his cap covered up his graying, sandy hair he looked younger than his forty years. The others in the unit had treated him like a harmless pervert, until one day, in the Ardennes, they had seen him kill two American soldiers with his bare hands. He was suspected of having derived some obscure sexual pleasure from the killings.

In Legge's own words he had been "exiled to Germany by his despairing family; had stayed on for the boys; and then for the Cause." It was absolutely true. Throughout the thirties Legge had been a remittance man in Berlin, supplementing his allowance by free-lance work for the Propaganda Ministry, and managing to survive the various purges against homosexuals.

The door opened.

"Well, well, well," O'Mara said, "if it isn't our old friend Captain Hellmann."

"Captain Hellmann," Legge said. "How lovely."

45

11

Deep in the Führerbunker was a small living room adjoining Hitler's study. Typical of the underground complex, it was a simple cell with whitewashed walls, and its stuffiness reflected the inadequacy of the air-conditioning system. The furniture consisted of one table, a sofa, and six armchairs. Hitler's closest associates were gathered there for the regular all-night vigil that the Führer's incurable insomnia demanded. The only face missing from the gathering was Eva Braun's. Eva Braun was a "non-person." She rarely left her own quarters.

Hanna Reitsch was sitting beside Hitler on the sofa. Goebbels and his wife were next to the army surgeon Dr. Stumpfegger. Bormann and General Burgdorf were talking in undertones. The two young secretaries were playing with Blondi, Hitler's Alsatian bitch.

Hanna Reitsch, the pretty test pilot once worshiped by the entire Luftwaffe, was trying to persuade Hitler to leave Berlin.

"Why stay here, my Führer? Why deprive the Reich of your irreplaceable person? You must live for the whole people—they're all asking for you."

For once this suggestion failed to trigger the usual temper tantrum. The bloodless lips moved with difficulty. "I've given orders to defend Berlin to the bitter end. My honor as a soldier demands that I remain here among my people. And I still have hope. Wenck may break through from the southeast and drive the Russians back across the Oder."

He turned to Frau Goebbels. "Where have your children gone, Magda? Are they tired of their Uncle Adolf? Is that why I don't hear them singing anymore? Where are Hela, Helmut, and little Hedda? Why haven't you brought them with you?"

"They've been put to bed, my Führer. They were so exhausted they nearly fell asleep at the supper table. But if you like, I'll send them to you in the morning."

"Hanna, listen carefully," Hitler said, turning back to the pilot. "I don't want you falling into the hands of the Russians. Here, take this."

He handed her an ampule containing a colorless liquid. "It's cyanide. Just a little pressure on the ampule and it's all over. Do you understand?"

"Are you certain it will work, my Führer?"

It was Bormann who had spoken, softly, from the other side of the room. Hitler was visibly shaken.

"What do you mean?"

"If the ampules should prove ineffective . . .? Where did we get them from?"

Bormann knew perfectly well that Himmler had supplied the cyanide. Hitler was aware of it, too. He was shifting uneasily on the sofa, his suspicion of his old friend Himmler obviously at work.

"Stumpfegger—what do you think?"

The doctor was startled. He pulled himself together

and said: "Perhaps, my Führer, it would be prudent to carry out a test."

"Well, *I'm* not going to be your guinea pig," Hanna said, in a desperate and forlorn attempt to lighten the atmosphere.

Hitler's head was sunk on his chest. Nobody spoke. The silence was unbearable. Then Hitler croaked: "Blondi."

The dog responded instantly to her master's voice, loping over to him, wagging her tail. Hitler took her collar, then nodded to Stumpfegger.

"Take her to Professor Haase. Instruct him and report to me."

Stumpfegger, white as the walls, led the dog out. Bormann took the opportunity of slipping out behind him.

Suddenly Hitler said: "Today I learned that there is a Ukrainian division in Berlin. The joke is that I knew absolutely nothing about it. Did you, Burgdorf?"

"I believe . . ." Burgdorf hesitated, seeking a tactful formula. "I believe that the Ukrainian division has been in Berlin some time."

"Was I told about it? I don't remember anyone telling me about it."

"Possibly not, my Führer."

Hitler fell silent. His eyes seemed to turn in. The people in the room knew what to expect: a rambling, disjointed monologue.

They listened, each occupied with his own thoughts, as Hitler's voice droned on and on. "The fundamental goal of my life, the whole reason for the genesis of National Socialism, the sole purpose of the war, has been the extirpation of Bolshevism. . . . But I have made mistakes. I have lacked ruthlessness. I have been too soft. I have been hampered by my allies. Mussolini. That posturing fool. Calling himself the Sword of Islam. Alienating our natural allies in the Arab world. . . . Time has defeated me. . . . So much to achieve, one miserable span of life to do it. . . . I have made mistakes. . . . I underestimated the power of the Jews over Churchill, that Yid-ridden half-American. . . . The English should have been my partners in the grand design. . . . I have been weak. Yes. And life forgives no weakness. . . ."

The monologue was interrupted by the reappearance of Stumpfegger.

"My Führer . . ."

Hitler understood. He rose and shuffled out of the room.

In one of the lavatories, Professor Haase, Hitler's veterinary surgeon, and Sergeant Tornow, his dog-handler, were standing over Blondi's body. Tornow was drunk. He had consumed the better part of a bottle of brandy, in five tremendous gulps, to enable him to carry out the Führer's unbelievable order. He had held Blondi, affectionate and trusting to the last, and forced her jaws open. Haase had placed the ampule in her mouth and had crushed it with a pair of pliers. Blondi had died almost instantly. One convulsion, a tiny whimper, and she was gone.

The door opened and Hitler came in. He stared down at Blondi's body for thirty or forty seconds, betraying not a trace of emotion, then turned abruptly and left.

"You must deal with Fraulein Braun's dogs. . . ."

"There's my own," Tornow said hoarsely.

"Use your pistol."

"I feel like using it on myself."

Hitler was meanwhile walking back to his study. He saw Bormann approaching and stopped. They were alone.

"Fenris," Bormann said. "I've just had confirmation from Prague. All is proceeding according to plan."

"Fenris?"

"Yes, my Führer . . ."

"Ah. Yes. Good." Hitler brightened suddenly. "Very good."

12

"You've seen them?" Vögler asked.

Hellmann nodded. It had been an unsettling encounter. Ward's menacing suspicion: "They've disarmed us, Hellmann. Why? Are you an employer or an executioner? We've had nothing but promises." O'Mara's sullen, brutal face, shapeless as a potato, topped with filthy, carrot-colored hair. Legge, the reincarnation of Fuchs-Jonesh. Chandra, oily, smiling. Duval, a little rat of a man, his deferential manner hiding God-knew-what resentments.

"They don't seem very enthusiastic," Vögler said.

"That's understandable. What about that Horch?"

"It's waiting for you."

"And weapons?" Wrack asked.

"Next door."

The three men crossed a corridor and entered a room with barred windows. It was the armory of the Kommandantur. Vögler indicated racks of automatic and semi-automatic weapons.

"Take your pick."

Wrack showed genuine enthusiasm. "Not bad, not bad at all." Almost lovingly, he picked up a Mauser M-1932 Schnellfeuer, a weapon issued exclusively to Waffen SS units.

"It's yours," said Vögler good-naturedly. "And as many clips as you want."

"Thanks, but I'll stick to a Schmeisser," Wrack said. "The Mauser's a fine weapon, but, for me, there's too much dispersion on a long burst."

He set the Mauser down and removed a fine 9 mm machine pistol from its rack. As coolly as an officer candidate undergoing an exam at Bad Tolz, Wrack withdrew the magazine and gave the breech two taps to be sure there was no live round in the chamber before unscrewing the barrel. He pressed a cam on the trigger housing, then gave it a quarter-turn to the right. He finished disassembling the piece by removing the bolt.

"It's in perfect condition," he announced after checking the well-oiled parts. "A real gem." He caressed the feeding mechanism with his fingertips. "Really a fine design. Two magazines can go side by side in firing position."

He reassembled the machine pistol, listening for the telltale click of the trigger as the bolt was seated. Then he tightened the assembly screw.

"I'll keep this."

"I'll take one, too," said Hellmann, selecting a similar weapon. Like Wrack, he disassembled the gun; a malfunction in combat could mean death.

"For the Englishmen, I had in mind Sten guns," Vögler said. "We've managed to put together quite a collection of Stens captured from the Czech resistance."

He unlocked another rack and spread out several models of the Enfield weapon, ranging from the crude, lightweight Sten MK-1 to the Sten MK-5, which could fire 550 rounds a minute.

"We also have Soviet 7.62 mm submachine guns and Czech ZK-383s."

"The Stens will do," Hellmann said.

"What the hell's this?" Wrack asked, indicating a rubber bag that contained the parts of a disassembled weapon.

Vögler grinned. "That's become a museum piece around here. It's American. They call it a .22 caliber repeating survival carbine. The Americans give them out to their Air Force men. Look, it can be taken down completely. The barrel is held by a single bolt. I don't know exactly where we got that one—in Italy or Greece probably."

"We're going to need grenades," Hellmann broke in. "And extra clips of ammunition. Also explosives, a dozen detonators, and a five-meter reel of cord."

Vögler whistled, impressed. "All right. Anything else?"

"I don't think so," Hellmann said. "Thanks for all your help."

An hour later Hellmann and Wrack led the five British Free Corps men and Stachek to the Horch truck. O'Mara was hefting his Sten lovingly, caressing it. Duval, an expert driver-mechanic, climbed in behind the wheel.

"Stachek, you'd better ride up front with me," Hellmann said.

Stachek nodded and handed Hellmann a packet. Hellmann hauled himself up into the truck and Stachek was about to follow when Wrack's voice rapped out.

"Just a moment."

Stachek's right foot was on the running board. Wrack's hand clamped onto his shoulder.

"Keep still," Wrack said.

Stachek shrugged and obeyed. Wrack searched him methodically, taking a heavy Luger from a pocket of his leather coat. Stachek said nothing, showed no emotion, but Hellmann could see rage in his eyes.

"Captain Hellmann," Wrack said, "may I know what he handed you a moment ago?"

Hellmann hesitated, wondering if it was the right moment to assert his authority over Wrack. He decided it was not.

"A *laissez-passer*. In case we should run into partisans."

"I see."

"Anything else you'd like to know . . . Lieutenant?"

"Divided they fall." Legge's languid voice came softly out of the darkness.

"Let's move it," Hellmann snapped.

"Come on. Move," Ward repeated.

Chandra, O'Mara, Legge, Ward, and Wrack piled into the back of the truck. Duval fired the engine and the truck ground out of the Kommandantur into the blacked-out streets.

13

Duval drove fast, despite the blue-dimmed headlights. Hellmann was impressed by the French Canadian's skill and avoided looking at the speedometer.

Stachek produced a packet of English cigarettes and offered one to Hellmann.

"Do you anticipate trouble up ahead?" Hellmann asked.

"It's not impossible, Captain."

"Partisans?"

"For the last two or three years, the partisans have been growing scarce in this region. Heydrich made things very hot for them and, after his assassination, their situation became untenable. Many of them joined the Yugoslav guerrillas, others holed up in the northeast. On the other hand, there are roving bands—foreign deserters from your army, Vlasov Ukrainians, even a few Germans."

"And the Wehrmacht allows them to organize?"

"The Wehrmacht has other fish to fry. In fact, the renegades even gave the army a hand clearing out villages where partisans were hiding. But they're a dangerous lot."

"You know them?"

"A little. Don't worry, Captain. Just trust me and you'll get where you're going."

Hellmann finished his cigarette, stretched his cramped legs, then swung himself over the seat and dropped down into the back of the truck.

"Everything all right?"

Cigarette ends glowed in the dark. The Horch bucked and jolted over the rough road.

"I'd like to know where we're going," Ward said. "And why."

There were murmurs of agreement.

"You'll be told. At the right time." Wrack's voice.

"I was addressing myself to Captain Hellmann," Ward said. Someone chuckled. Legge, Hellmann thought.

"We've been given some very extravagant promises, Captain Hellmann," Ward went on. "If they're genuine, they imply a mission of some seriousness—and danger. Is it really wise to keep us in the dark? In my experience men fight better in daylight."

"As Lieutenant Wrack has said, you will be told at the right time. It's nearly sunup. Be on the alert."

The words were hardly out of his mouth when Duval hissed: "Captain. Men on the road. Up ahead."

Hellmann heard the clicks of safety catches and magazines being snapped into machine pistols. As he vaulted into the front, snapping off his own safety catch, he felt reassured. Ward's men might be mutinous and treacherous, but they were professional.

"All right. Slow down," he said to Duval. The Horch began to lose speed.

Ahead, in the misty dawn, stood a motley band of

men, with arms and uniforms borrowed from at least four nations.

"I count six," Hellmann said. "Stachek?"

"Yes," the Czech said. "But they'll have maybe twenty, thirty in the trees."

"Obviously."

Hellmann felt Wrack's breath on his ear. "Run the bastards down."

Hellmann ignored him. He reached under the seat and brought out a parcel, wrapped in newspaper. He handed the parcel to Stachek.

"Will it work?" he said.

Stachek grinned. "Guaranteed."

The Czech climbed out of the truck onto the road. He held his arms high to indicate that he was unarmed. He walked slowly toward the partisan leader, a big man, with a tangle of reddish beard, who wore a Wehrmacht greatcoat and a fur hat.

"Rolf—it's Stachek."

Rolf's teeth showed briefly in the bluish light of the Horch's head lamps.

"We'll buy our way through," Stachek said.

"With what? Guns? Alcohol?"

"Better than that, Rolf. Here." He offered the parcel.

Rolf lowered the muzzle of his submachine gun slightly. After a moment he took the parcel, unwrapped the newspaper, and examined the contents.

"What are you trying to pull?"

The tone of Rolf's voice made his men tense their trigger fingers. The others, hiding in the brush, stirred, and Stachek detected the click of a machine pistol being cocked.

"It's better than gold," Stachek said calmly. "Penicillin. I've got more under refrigeration."

"Where did you get it?"

Stachek hesitated a moment, then said: "My reward for guiding this truck to Germany."

"How much more have you got?"

"Thousands of doses. I'll go fifty-fifty with you."

"In exchange for what?"

"Protection. You've got enough men and influence around here to make sure that nothing happens to me."

"All right. What's in the truck that's worth thousands of doses of penicillin?"

"I don't know." Stachek buttoned his long leather military coat, turned up the collar, and buried his hands in the pockets. "I don't know. What does it matter? I'll be back in two, three days."

"Make sure you are. Remember, we've made a deal."

"I'll remember."

Rolf signaled to his men and they started to melt away. By the time Stachek was back in the truck, the road was deserted.

"Was that bearded one German?" Hellmann asked as Duval shifted into gear and stepped on the throttle.

"Rolf? Yes, he's German all right," Stachek said. "A Wehrmacht noncom. He deserted to be with his wife again and got picked up by the Feldgendarmerie. He was actually sentenced to death, but managed to break away—with the handcuffs still on him. He'd rather wait out the end of the war in these woods than go back and be strung up from some lamppost or meat hook in the back of a butcher's shop. I've known him for nearly a year now. He's clever. A man with a future."

"Uh-huh." Hellmann settled back in his seat, then asked: "Are we going to run into many more of these people?"

"No. It's nearly daylight and the American planes

always come at dawn. They fly just above the trees and strafe anything that moves. If you want to go on south you'll have to find another way. Just how far do you plan to go?"

Hellmann did not answer him. He turned his head. "You men in the back, try to get some rest. We're going to be rolling for another two hours, then we leave the truck. You all right, Duval?"

Duval nodded.

Hellmann shifted to get comfortable and began to doze. Then he slept. He slept for a long time but it seemed like only a moment between drifting off and Stachek waking him.

"Germany," he said. The truck was approaching a fork in the road. "Munich is a hundred kilometers to the southwest. If you want my advice, Captain, you'll give me the Horch. I'll drive it back to the Kommandantur."

Hellmann turned to speak to Wrack.

"We'll have to carry our gear until we spot a less conspicuous vehicle. The Americans have their forward elements all over this sector. We don't want to run into a Sherman tank. We'll find a place to ditch the Horch and Stachek can drive it back to Brno after dark."

Duval soon spotted a clearing and backed the Horch under a canopy of overhanging branches. One after the other, the men jumped over the tailgate of the truck. Hellmann noticed that Wrack positioned himself somewhat to the rear of the others, his Schmeisser cradled in his arm.

"Why leave the truck?" he said. "We'll lose time."

"But we'll stay alive."

Wrack shrugged. "You're in command. But if we have to continue on foot, there is one matter to be settled."

"What's that?"

"Him." Wrack jerked his chin at Stachek. "This mission can succeed only if we take every possible precaution. If the truck stays, he stays."

The sixth sense of a born survivor saved Stachek. He dived for the bushes seconds before Wrack's finger squeezed the trigger of his Schmeisser.

Stachek somersaulted into a ditch, Wrack's bullets stuttering over his head. Then he was up and running. A second burst of fire tore bark off the trees near him. He staggered as lead ripped through his shoulder, then recovered and raced on, deep into the forest.

Wrack was ejecting his empty clip, cramming in a fresh one.

Instinct made Hellmann level his own weapon.

"You crazy bastard."

Suddenly he knew he had to kill Wrack.

"That's enough. Drop your weapons." Ward's words were as sharp as gunshots. "Drop them."

Hellmann dragged his eyes away from Wrack's. Ward had deployed his men in a circle round him and Wrack. Five Stens were trained on them.

O'Mara was directly behind Wrack, and moving toward him. Hellmann dropped his Schmeisser. Wrack's face was as taut as a hawser. He was going to fire. Hellmann knew it.

"Go on," O'Mara said quietly, pressing the muzzle of his Sten behind Wrack's ear. "It'd make my day."

Very gradually Wrack relaxed. His Schmeisser dropped onto the rain-soaked moss.

O'Mara lowered his Sten and stepped back.

"Now," Ward said. "Let's have some answers. Where are we going and what is the mission?"

Wrack answered him, his voice perfectly level. "You

have been promised money and new identity papers. I am the only one who knows where they are." He jerked his head at Hellmann. "He knows nothing."

Ward turned to Hellmann.

"It's true," Hellmann said.

"I see."

Ward glanced inquiringly at Legge. Legge shrugged. "Honors appear to be even," he said.

"I want to know what the hell we're getting into," O'Mara said.

"So do I," said Ward. "Listen, Wrack, you need us just as much as we need you. Very well. We'll do what we have to do. But you're going to tell us what that is. Right now."

"I am not authorized to reveal any information until we reach our destination."

"The mission," Hellmann said, "is to locate ex-Reichsmarschall Hermann Göring and execute him." Ignoring Wrack's ferocious look, he went on. "We are acting under the direct orders of the Führer and Martin Bormann. Göring has been sentenced to death. Our duty is to carry out that sentence."

There was a stunned silence. Hellmann turned to Wrack. "There's no point in concealing the facts."

There was a sneer on Wrack's lips. "Your conduct will be reported to Bormann himself," he said. "You can be sure of that."

"Where is Göring?" Ward said.

Hellmann answered him. "Not far from here. At Mauterndorf. He's being held by a detachment of SS. They may be willing to hand him over, or they may not. In any case, our mission is to liquidate him."

"To get to Mauterndorf we have to cross American lines," Chandra said.

There was another silence, eventually broken by Legge.

"Not *this* boy," he said.

"That goes for me," Duval said. "Jesus Christ."

"This isn't a mission, Captain Hellmann," Ward said. "It's suicide."

"I don't think so," Hellmann said. "I think we have a reasonable chance of success. In any case, it is your only chance of getting out of Germany. Lieutenant Wrack, I think it would be helpful if you explained the arrangements that have been made."

Wrack frowned at him for a moment, then said: "There is a hunting lodge somewhere between Mauterndorf and Radstadt. Two agents of the Race and Resettlement Office are there now. They will wait for us for as long as is necessary. They have two thousand pounds for each one of you and forged German and Swedish papers. They will hand you over to a chain of *passeurs* who will smuggle you across the Italian border and from there into Spain."

"And what," O'Mara said, "if you stop a bit of lead between here and Mauterndorf?"

Wrack smiled thinly. "It is very much in the interest of all of you that I should not."

"Wrack's right," Hellmann said. "Your only chance of survival rests in him—and in the successful completion of the mission. My job is to lead you to Mauterndorf. My responsibility ends when Göring has been killed."

O'Mara raised his Sten, a grin splitting his face. "Well now, I think I could think of a few ways of persuading Lieutenant Wrack to tell us what we want to know without going to the trouble of dodging Sherman tanks all the way to Mauterndorf. You'd give us a hand, wouldn't you, Legge? You know where it hurts a man."

Hellmann, against his will, had to admire the coolness with which Wrack replied: "But you would have no means of knowing if I was telling you the truth."

Hellmann reflected that in Wrack's case total ruthlessness was combined with courage; so often it was a mask for cowardice.

"I propose we vote on it," said Ward. "Do we proceed with the mission or not? Chandra?"

"On balance—yes," Chandra said.

"Duval?"

"I guess we don't have a lot of choice."

"Legge?"

"I concur. Under protest."

"O'Mara?"

"Well," the Irishman said. "I'm really rather looking forward to it. Will you let me kill Göring, Captain? It'd be something to tell my grandchildren."

Hellmann stooped and picked up his Schmeisser. Nobody attempted to stop him.

"Now that we've lost Stachek," said Hellmann, "we'll have to camouflage the Horch. We'll move on foot until we find a vehicle to replace it—preferably an American one. The situation in this sector is still confused. We stand an excellent chance of getting through to Mauterndorf."

Ward detailed Chandra, Duval, and O'Mara to start cutting branches and underbrush to hide the Horch, then walked over to Hellmann. He produced one of his rare smiles.

"If you could vote on your future, Captain Hellmann," he said, "I wonder which way you'd go."

Stachek had doubled back on his own trail when no one had followed to finish him off. He had crawled nearly fifty meters despite the agony in his shoulder. He had reached the edge of the clearing, only a stone's throw from the Horch, just as Hellmann had started to explain the mission. If he had been armed, he would certainly have killed Wrack then and there. Opting for prudence, he merely listened with increasing wonder and excitement. The information was worth a fortune if he could do business with the right party—Göring himself, his SS guards, or the advancing Americans. But as a member of the USB he was a hunted man. He had to find a protector—and quickly. He thought of Rolf and his men, but dismissed the idea as risky. The Americans then. Their intelligence service was rich and powerful. He'd get medical treatment, and sanctuary, even if it meant losing his freedom temporarily.

When Hellmann led his men out of the clearing, Stachek had decided. He would give himself up to the first American unit he met. And somehow he would engineer a further encounter with Lieutenant Wrack.

14

APRIL 28, 1945, 9:00 A.M.

Göring thought he had lost weight. He was admiring himself in his bedroom mirror, almost convinced that the glass reflected the glamorous young fighter pilot who had taken command of the von Richthofen squadron in 1918. It was some compensation for the depressed state he was in, as a result of being denied his pills. After twenty-four hours without codeine, he had lost his natural optimism and good nature. This morning, as he got out of his canopied bed, his dizzy spells had returned and he had been forced to lie down again for nearly a quarter of an hour. His wife came in, accompanied by Emil.

"I'll cut quite a reasonable figure when I meet Eisenhower," he said. "The only problem is the uniform—I can't make up my mind."

"I wouldn't worry about your uniform," his wife said dryly. "Come and have breakfast. General Koller's waiting downstairs."

"Koller? I thought he'd left for Berlin yesterday."

"Apparently all air corridors have been cut. He had to turn back."

The dining hall of Mauterndorf Castle was vast and

64

lugubrious. Low-ceilinged, with great, hand-hewn beams, the room was decorated with suits of armor. A long fire roared in the fireplace despite the spring sunshine outside. Three Luftwaffe officers were seated at the vast table. They rose as Göring entered.

"Koller! Grumann! Reinecke!" said Göring heartily. "So, Koller, you couldn't go to Berlin—despite the Führer's orders?"

"Unfortunately not, Herr Marschall. I got as far as Fechlin. They said it was impossible to fly into Berlin. Even Gatow Airport has come under Soviet artillery fire. Berlin is a trap—nothing gets in, nothing gets out. But I managed to speak to Hanna Reitsch on the telephone. Von Greim, too."

"And so?"

"Von Greim advised me to stay where I was. As for Hanna, she seemed so overwrought that I hung up."

"I always thought that woman was a crank and a fanatic," Göring commented as he took a seat at the table.

His wife left the room, the officers sat down again, and Koller glanced around warily.

"How are they behaving with you, Herr Marschall?"

"Who? The SS?"

"Yes."

Göring shrugged and looked sourly at the vegetable stew that was all that had been provided for his breakfast.

"They've been reasonably correct. Except for that drunken swine Kaltenbrunner."

"Is he here?"

"He's gone, thank God. He was here yesterday. Walked all over the castle without saying a word. Then he went away, leaving the stink of bad schnapps in his wake. A little while later, the Gauleiter of the Oberdonau turned up—that Eigruber fellow. Do you know what that worm dared to say?"

"What?"

"That country bumpkin informed me—in front of my wife, my daughter, *and* the servants—that anyone who opposed the Führer in his district would be placed before a firing squad, regardless of rank."

Koller looked suitably shocked. "Does he have the power to do that?"

"How the hell should I know?" Göring suddenly pounded his fist on the table. "When I think what the Führer owes me! I was one of the first to join that . . . that third-rate adventurer, and now look at how he treats me! I introduced him to high society when he was just a local rabble-rouser who didn't have a spare shirt to his name. And he dares to call me a traitor! I introduced him to ministers, industrialists, generals."

"Herr Marschall, please . . ." Koller had no intention of being compromised with the war almost over. The door burst open and Koller knocked over his mug of coffee. But it was only Emil, panting and sweating.

"Luftwaffe parachutists!" Emil gasped. "A whole detachment landing in the park."

Göring leaped to his feet. "Luftwaffe—my own Luftwaffe," he cried exultantly. "Now we shall see, by God. Now we shall see!"

15

The farm buildings formed a U. On one side of the farmhouse were stables and pigsties; on the other, lean-to sheds and the hayloft.

Surrounding the farm the broad panorama of the countryside was divided by a dirt road which, starting from the beaten-earth courtyard, left the farm to intersect with the paved road a hundred meters down the hillside. All around the property lay cultivated fields bordered from west to northwest by a grove of trees belonging to the farm and representing the farthest advance of the forest.

The morning mist was dissipating rapidly, heralding a sunny day. The stable door opened and a tall, broad-shouldered woman, in her forties, appeared. With her full-blown figure and her graying blond hair, drawn back tightly over her skull, she was the picture of wholesome good health. She held the heavy wooden door open a few seconds, just long enough to allow a man who looked about fifteen years her junior to carry out two brimming pails of warm, frothy milk. When the barn door had closed behind them, the man and woman crossed the courtyard side by side, talking in a curious mixture of French and German, laughing at every other remark. In contrast to her dirndl skirt and fresh white peasant blouse, the lean, rawboned man trudged along in wooden shoes and wore a shapeless jacket marked down the back with the letters KG—Kriegsgefangene.

"*Eh bien*, Pierre, the life of a prisoner of war here is not so bad, *nicht wahr?*"

He lowered his pails to the ground with a smile, but the woman seemed to back away.

"Not here, Pierre. She can see."

"*Et alors?* She knows all about us."

He shoved a dog away with the toe of his wooden shoe and, looking up at the front of the farmhouse, thought he saw one of the lacy curtains move in the upstairs bedroom window.

"Your daughter doesn't like me very much, Trudi. How much longer am I going to have to sleep in the shed?"

She gave him a gap-toothed smile and tossed her head. She was about to answer him when a rumble from the road echoed against the ivy-covered walls, filling the courtyard with noise. The woman blinked, then instinctively moved behind Pierre. Apprehensively the Frenchman watched as an armored half-track ground through the gate and lurched to a halt in the middle of the courtyard, scattering poultry and dogs.

The white-starred M-16, a reconnaissance vehicle, had a crew of eight. Six of them manned the four .50 caliber machine guns mounted on the turret. Stowed under a tarpaulin at the rear of the scout car was an odd assemblage of ammunition boxes, cases of rations, crates of German beer. On the righthand door of the cab was stenciled CALAMITY JANE and a slogan painted in white: GERMANY KAPUT!

"Americans!" the woman whispered.

She began fussing with her blouse and then tucked in a wisp of gray-blond hair that had escaped from her bun. Her face showed a mixture of embarrassment and pleasure as the soldiers nudged one another to get a better look. One leering GI gave her a wolf whistle. Pierre stood sullenly observing his liberators.

The officer seated beside the driver opened his door and jumped out athletically. He was one of those young second lieutenants that the U.S. Army seemed to have in limitless quantities. Under a helmet two sizes too large, he smiled boyishly. Watching him move, Pierre thought that his walk was patterned after the cowboys in western films. And the Colt .45 rode far lower on his slim hips than regulations allowed, making the boy officer look even more like a celluloid hero. Meanwhile three enlisted men climbed down from the back of the vehicle, leaving only three to man the machine guns.

In halting German the Second Lieutenant asked for some water and, pointing at the chickens that had returned to peck at corn a few yards away, said he wanted to buy some of them.

Without waiting for her reply, three of the GIs started chasing one of the hens, to the encouraging shouts of the men on the turret.

"We will pay," the young officer continued, offering several army-issue occupation marks and some dollars.

The German woman took the money and slipped it into a pocket of her skirt.

"Quick, Pierre, bring the pails into the kitchen and then help them."

"Go to the devil!" he answered, kicking over the pails of milk.

The young Lieutenant's smile faded. He turned to

watch his men climbing back onto the half-track, holding two or three captured hens by the legs.

"Pierre!" the big woman hissed as the Frenchman strode away to the shed where his belongings were kept.

She smiled winningly at the American officer.

"You take him . . . away with you?"

The American shrugged. As he opened his mouth to reply the woman saw the smooth, boyish face disintegrate like a melon dropped onto a road. A tenth of a second later she heard the shots.

Twin arcs of lead swept the courtyard and one of the GIs spun crazily, threw up his hands, and went sprawling facedown in mud. Another blinked in astonishment as a bloodstain spread across the front of his fatigue jacket. A third started to run and was cut down by a burst of machine-gun fire. Instants later the three men manning the guns died. Then there was silence.

At the first shots, Pierre had come running from the shed. With bullets splattering mud at his heels, he'd managed to cross the courtyard alive and reach the woman. He had seized her arm and pulled her toward the barn.

When a grenade dropped in front of them, he instinctively stooped to seize it, yelling: "Run!"

The grenade killed him the next second and left the woman a dismembered corpse. Grenades rained into the farmyard, blowing the barn door off its hinges. Flying shrapnel decimated the chickens and ricocheted off the armor of the half-track. The blasts shook the very foundations of the farmhouse, shattering windows. Then silence again. From beneath a wagon one of the dogs howled.

Minutes went by without anything moving in the courtyard. Then a slate tinkled down from the roof of the barn and crouching figures appeared against the skyline.

They dropped down from the roof into the yard. Three others advanced cautiously.

"Firework night," said Legge.

Hellmann turned over the Second Lieutenant's body with his toe. Duval was staring with horror at what was left of the woman.

"Carnage," Ward said.

"Necessary," said Wrack. "We can't take prisoners and there must be no witnesses. We have the vehicle we were looking for."

"And the uniforms," Hellmann added.

"You mean we've got to wear them?" asked Chandra. The idea appalled him.

"I'm afraid so," Hellmann said.

O'Mara spat. "I see one that'll fit me a treat."

Hellmann pointed to the half-track.

"We'll have to clean it up. If we passed another vehicle from the same unit, they'd spot a name like Calamity Jane. All markings must be scraped off and painted over."

"We might rechristen her 'Lili Marlene'," Legge suggested.

"You just volunteered," Hellmann said. He turned to Duval. "Can you handle her?"

Duval climbed up into the driver's seat and played with the gearshift.

"No problem," he said. "It's one of the latest models. They took the standard 1943 chassis and converted it into the M-16."

"You've seen these before?"

"Nothing on wheels I haven't seen. This is one of the best—made in Detroit. Transverse torsion bars and six wheels on each side. She'll do up to forty-five miles an hour—"

"All right, Duval," Ward broke in. "We'll take your word for it. Get working with Legge. I want all those markings off. Chandra, O'Mara, go into the house and see if you can find some food and drink."

He turned to Hellmann and Wrack. "Shall we do the dirty work?"

Chandra and O'Mara crossed the yard to the door of the farmhouse. They burst into a little kitchen with a black cast-iron range and tiled floors. Duval pulled open drawers and rummaged through cupboards while O'Mara cautiously opened the door to the adjoining room.

"I'll check upstairs," O'Mara said.

Chandra nodded and placed his Sten on the blue-and-white checkered tablecloth, took a glass from the cupboard, and filled it with fresh water from the sink. He drained the glass at a single gulp, filled it again, then noticed the framed photographs on the shelf. Glass in hand, he went closer.

The first photograph, draped with black crepe, showed the square face of a Bavarian peasant dressed in a Wehrmacht engineer corps uniform. *"Egon to Trudi, 1942"* was the inscription. The second photograph showed a teen-age girl standing between her parents in the courtyard of the farm. *"Egon, Trudi, and Erika, July 1941."* Fourteen plus four, thought Chandra, she must be a good-looking girl now. He admired the slender legs, slim waist, and precociously heavy breasts.

The stairs disappeared in the semidarkness of a short corridor filled with the odor of floor wax and furniture polish. O'Mara stopped on the last step, listening for the slightest sound. The floor creaked under his weight and he moved slightly, his Sten at the ready, his finger on the trigger. The shadowy light in the corridor came from a tiny skylight and he spotted two doors to his left, two to his right. His back to the wall, O'Mara moved forward and pushed open the first door, ready to jump back at the slightest movement. Nothing happened and he looked inside cautiously.

It was a little dressing room with a wall mirror, shelves, a pitcher and a basin made of blue-and-white porcelain, and piles of clean towels.

O'Mara inspected the room carefully and closed the door again. Hugging the wall, he moved to the second door, taking the same precautions. This time he found a shadowy room whose dormer windows were shuttered and covered with curtains. His eyes by now accustomed to the semidarkness, he inspected the room before withdrawing. Then he crossed the hall and opened the third door.

This room was flooded with sunlight despite its curtains. O'Mara ran his eyes over the room, noting the meticulously clean wooden floor, the shelves which held a few leather-bound books and pots of geraniums, and a built-in cupboard in the corner. He was about to retreat when he heard a floorboard creak.

He froze for a moment. Then a slow smile spread across his face. He ran his fingers through the greasy, carroty curls of his hair, and started to advance very slowly toward the cupboard.

His Sten leveled, he wrenched open the cupboard door.

The girl was huddled on the floor, her knees drawn up to her chin, hugging herself. Two round, terrified eyes, red-rimmed from crying, stared up at O'Mara.

"Well, well, well," O'Mara said in a half-whisper.

"Come out of there and let's take a look at you."

The girl didn't understand English, but the jerking movement of O'Mara's Sten was unmistakable. Trembling violently, she struggled to her feet and stepped out of the cupboard.

She was beautiful. Her hair was long and blond. Her simple cotton dress, moist with her sweat, clung to her, revealing well-formed breasts and an hourglass figure.

"Don't kill me. Please."

O'Mara understood her German. He put a finger to his lips and said: "Sssh."

Some of the terror drained from the girl's eyes.

"Name. Name," O'Mara said.

"Erika."

"Erika," he repeated. He smiled.

She read his smile. She nodded. She put her hands on her breasts, her expression clearly implying: "Is this what you want?"

O'Mara's mouth was suddenly dry. Again putting a finger to his lips, he laid his Sten on a chair. He turned back to the girl and made her kneel in front of him.

"Jesus God," O'Mara murmured as he felt her nervous fingers obediently undoing the buttons of his trousers.

Chandra had found a store of cheeses, bread, liver sausage, and bottles of wine. He was making a pile of provisions on the kitchen table.

Hellmann came in. He nodded approvingly.

"In the countryside they always live well," Chandra said. "In Europe, at least. In India it is more usually the other way round."

"Where's O'Mara?"

"Investigating upstairs."

Hellmann picked up a glass and was moving toward the sink when a girl's piercing shriek of agony ripped through the house.

"Stay here," Hellmann rapped at Chandra. Flinging away the glass, he ran into the next room. Shriek after shriek reverberated as Hellmann took the narrow stairs three at a time.

He passed two empty rooms and kicked open the door of the third.

The girl was spread-eagled on the bed, facedown. O'Mara, naked from the waist down, was on top of her, grunting with mingled effort and pleasure.

Drawing his heavy Schmeisser, Hellmann took three strides across the room. He raised his arm, then chopped down. The butt of the pistol connected with the back of O'Mara's head. The Irishman's body went slack. The girl's sobs and wails filled the room.

Hellmann thought: I hope I've killed the animal.

16

APRIL 28, 1945, 12:30 P.M.

An elementary-school building near Mühldorf served as temporary headquarters for the Thirty-sixth Division's G-2 section. This particular HQ covered only the forward elements; the men in charge of military intelligence for the division were still twenty-five miles to the rear.

The school included a tiny courtyard that the Americans had sandbagged. In the building itself were two classrooms separated by a corridor. In each, the chairs had been piled in a corner to make more room and the childish drawings once thumbtacked to the walls had now given way to military maps. One room was being used for interrogation of prisoners while the other served as an office for the intelligence officer in command.

The noonday sun flooded through the bay windows and Captain Abernathy was eating lunch with Sergeant T/4 DiSalvo. The two men were seated at the schoolmaster's desk, which stood on a dais at the end of the room. They were working very hard at chewing the tough meat that had come from the mobile field kitchen.

"Stinkin' meat loaf," Di Salvo said. "Don't the cook know anythin' else?"

"Don't even know how to bake meat loaf," Abernathy said sourly, reaching for a bottle of German beer.

"I'll go for the coffee," DiSalvo said.

Outside, in the sunlit courtyard, a dozen men sat leaning against the sandbags, talking cheerfully as they ate their rations. DiSalvo walked toward the field-kitchen truck, wondering whether you only acquired taste buds with a sergeant's stripes.

Alone in the classroom, Abernathy lit a short, ropy Italian cigar DiSalvo had given him. He swung his feet onto the desk, leaned back in his chair, and stared at the big map on the opposite wall. The legend read: *Unconfirmed Installations Within the Reported Redoubt Zone.*

He scowled. That huge rectangle of paper was his nemesis. It was a detailed enlargement of a region covering the alpine sectors of Bavaria, western Austria, and northern Italy. In the center of the map, the name *Berchtesgaden* had been written and, right beside it, a second name, *Obersalzberg*. The first referred to Hitler's former residence; the second, a peak over two thousand meters high.

"The reported redoubt," Abernathy said out loud. "Reported—by who?"

He got to his feet and planted himself in front of the map, which had been sent through from SHAEF a month before. Red semicircles, triangles, tridents, figures, and letters indicated possible caches of foodstuffs, ammunition, gasoline, and poison gas. Radio installations, underground barracks, and HQ bunkers were shown as either already existing or under construction. Lines of fortifications designated by code names appeared either as solid black or dotted lines. If the information contained on this map proved accurate, the region would constitute the most powerful natural fortress ever employed by a warring nation. Abernathy drew on his cigar and went back to the desk.

"What a lousy assignment," he muttered to himself. "Why me? One man to clean out the whole goddamned Alpenfestung!"

He opened one of the desk drawers and removed a copy of the document said to be Eisenhower's favorite reading material. The document was in a green ring binder marked "Top Priority." It bore the same title as the map: "Unconfirmed Installations Within the Reported Redoubt Zone." The binder also contained an OSS report dated September 1944, as well as a document from the War Department and copies of telegrams sent by Allied agents working in Switzerland. The long report attached to the file had been written more recently—only a month before—by the commanding officer of the Seventh Army's G-2 section and referred to possible concentrations of troops and material—"200,000 to 300,000 SS and Alpenjäger"—in the region of the national redoubt.

If it was true, Abernathy reflected for the umpteenth time, the damned war would last another ten years.

He finished his beer and dropped his cigar butt into the bottle. The classroom door opened and DiSalvo reappeared, a tin mug of coffee in each hand. From the hallway behind him came heavy footfalls and shouting.

"What the hell's going on out there?" Abernathy demanded.

"Our recon boys from Charlie Company picked up some guy ten miles north of here. He flagged them down and said he had something highly confidential. But he'd only tell a high-ranking officer. The patrol brought him back here and now he's kickin' up a row because he wants to go back to G-2 in the rear."

"What is he—a Kraut?"

"I don't think so. He's wearing civilian clothes. Speaks German with a weird accent. Zelazny says he could be Hungarian or Czech."

"Another clown trying to save his neck. Maybe an SS deserter. I'll go and take a look at him."

"They're giving him first aid."

"What's wrong with him?"

"Wounded, but not bad. Bullet went right through a muscle without hitting bone."

Abernathy made his way to the interrogation room. A powerful odor of antiseptic met him as he opened the door. He went over to a half-opened window and waited while two corpsmen from HQ finished bandaging the newcomer. In one corner, a GI sucked a matchstick, his carbine pointed negligently at the prisoner.

"That should do it," the medic said, collecting his instruments and putting them into his bag. He and his assistant left, tossing Abernathy a careless salute. Abernathy nodded to the guard, who ambled out on the heels of the medics.

Alone with the man, Abernathy pulled up a chair and straddled it, his elbows resting on its back. For a moment, the two men regarded each other in silence. The civilian was a powerful, brutal-looking man. His expression was sullen—but Abernathy sensed relief mixed with apprehension. Interesting.

"You speak English?"

"Not good. I'm better in German," he added in that language.

"Okay," said Abernathy, who was a natural linguist

79

and had made a point of learning German: "First of all, who are you and what is your nationality?"

"I've already told your men that I want to see the commanding officer of this division."

"I know. Listen, my friend, you're at an advanced outpost. There is a brigadier general and a major general over me, but they have their own jobs. The chain of command goes through me, right? Again: who are you and where do you come from?"

"My name is Stachek. I'm Czech."

"Did you serve in the German Army?"

"No . . ." The Czech hesitated. "I was in the USB."

"I see. So they won't exactly put the flags out for you in your own country."

"Which is why I've surrendered to you. I haven't come empty-handed. I have a secret that I'm sure your intelligence people would like to share."

"Yeah?" Abernathy was deliberately skeptical.

"It concerns a very high-ranking Nazi dignitary. He would be second or third on your list of most-wanted war criminals."

"Which one?"

"Göring."

Stachek expected a reaction. He was disappointed.

"He's hiding in this region," he went on. "You'll have to work fast if you want him alive. Hitler has sentenced him to death and an assault group has been assigned the task of executing him. They're on their way already."

"Are they the ones who shot you?"

Stachek nodded. "I was their guide. One of them wanted me out of the way. An SS bastard. There's something else that should interest you. The group is led by two Germans. But the rest are British Waffen SS."

"Say that again?"

Stachek repeated it, and at last he was rewarded with a reaction. Abernathy rose and started pacing.

"Okay," he said. "Give it to me again. All the details you've got."

17

Göring had been confined to the kitchens of Castle Mauterndorf. And for once in his life he was indifferent to the aromas of meat and sauces. Upstairs his fate was being decided. With him were his wife, his daughter, a maid, a cook, Emil, General Koller, and his two adjutants. At the top of the stairs that led to the kitchen a young SS soldier was on guard.

"If only we knew what was happening!" Göring whined. "This is unendurable. Do you know what's going on, Emil?"

Emil shrugged. "I talked to one of the parachutists. They mean to do something, but exactly what I don't know."

"We can't stay cooped up in here all day," Göring's wife said. "We don't even have a bathroom. It's revolting!"

General Koller was beginning to regret having put his head into the lion's mouth; he would have given anything to be somewhere else—anywhere else.

"You, down there! *Move!*"

The voice from the top of the stairs startled them. In the semidarkness Göring made out the skinny officer who had confiscated his codeine. He shuddered. Orders must have arrived from Berlin. It was all over.

Göring climbed the stairs laboriously, followed by his companions. They were led into the great baronial hall where they had eaten breakfast a few hours before. Fifteen apprehensive-looking SS men stood around.

The senior officer marched up to Göring. His manner was hostile, but the Reichsmarschall sensed that he was frightened.

"The Luftwaffe parachutists are demanding that I hand you over to them. But the Führer himself placed you under our guard."

Göring glimpsed hope for the second time that day. The SS officer wasn't certain of himself. It was a situation requiring tact and diplomacy—and a show of authority.

"I know nothing of any parachutists," Göring said. "What are they doing here?"

"I assumed that you had summoned them."

"But you know yourself that I haven't left the castle for days."

The officer barked out some orders. His men moved to the windows and doors. He turned to Göring again.

"I am responsible directly to the Führer."

"Do you intend to open fire on the Luftwaffe?"

"If necessary."

"Major, several times in the last two days you have called me a traitor to my face. But I have never ordered one German soldier to kill another. German fighting German with the enemies of the Reich not twenty kilometers away! That's what I call treason, Major. I am a Marschall of the German Reich and I will not, *will not* permit it."

Göring glanced at the Major's men. They were listening, and they were impressed. He could read that in their faces. So could the Major, who cleared his throat uneasily.

"Herr Reichsmarschall . . ." he began. Göring cut him short.

"Order your men to open fire on their comrades. See if they will obey that order."

The Major moistened his lips. "Let me speak to the commanding officer of the Luftwaffe detachment," Göring said. "This matter must be settled without bloodshed."

The Major hesitated. He looked at his men again. He decided. "Very well. Under the circumstances I feel I would be fulfilling my duty in permitting it."

Göring nodded. He marched purposefully to the door. The SS guard stood aside.

As he strode into the sunlit courtyard of the castle he was greeted with loud cheers and hurrahs by the Luftwaffe men. They crowded round him. Göring beamed, shook hands, slapped shoulders.

The senior officer snapped to attention and saluted smartly.

"Adjutant. I am delighted to see you," Göring said. "Your name is . . . ?"

"Adjutant Aviator Kohnle, Herr Reichsmarschall."

Göring took him by the arm, in the most friendly fashion, and drew him aside.

"Tell me, Kohnle," he said, lowering his voice, excited, "who ordered you to rescue me? Henschler? Von Lehr?"

Kohnle looked confused. "Our arrival was . . . pure chance, Herr Reichsmarschall. Our unit is heading for Radstadt. Near Zell-am-See. Our fool of a navigator mistook the drop zone. When we heard you were here, under arrest . . ."

Göring was staring at him. Then he burst into a roar of laughter. He clapped Kohnle on the shoulder.

"You were sent by fate," he said. "The stars are fighting for me."

18

"It's up to you, Captain Hellmann," Ward said.

O'Mara was sitting on the step of the half-track, nursing his head. The others stood round in a circle, Erika close to Hellmann. The corpses of the GIs had been laid out in a row in the corner of the yard. Naked except for their drab olive-green underwear, they looked pitiful.

"My personal inclination is to have him shot," Hellmann said.

"I'm terribly shocked, O'Mara," Legge said, and then turned to Hellmann. "But if every man who favored sodomy were to be shot, the world would be depopulated."

"The incident is trivial," Wrack said. "We need every man we've got. We're wasting time."

"Very well," Hellmann said. He turned to O'Mara. "If you try anything of the kind again, O'Mara, you *will* be shot. By me. Personally."

O'Mara looked up. It was obvious that he was totally unrepentant. He touched the back of his head.

"I'll remember you said that, Captain. I've got plenty to remind me of you."

Hellmann ignored him. He indicated the pile of American uniforms. "Everybody get changed. Move."

"Just a moment," Ward said. "What about the girl? What are we going to do with her?"

"She cannot be left behind," Wrack said.

"Oh dear," Legge said, in an undertone, "there goes another one."

"I agree," Hellmann said to Wrack, ignoring Legge. "Which is why she's coming with us."

Wrack's eyes were colder than ever. "American Army reconnaissance vehicles don't carry female, civilian passengers. You take her and you endanger the entire operation."

"He's got a point," Ward said.

"We have more uniforms than we need. She can have one."

Hellmann hefted his Sten. He wanted Wrack to know that he was prepared to kill if there was any further objection.

"Having saved her from a fate worse than death, it really would seem rather perverse to kill her," Legge said.

85

Ward smiled, and there were chuckles from some of the others.

"Very well," Wrack said. "But I repeat. In my opinion you are jeopardizing the mission."

"Let's get on with it," Hellmann said.

They stripped off their Wehrmacht uniforms and pulled on GI-issue fatigue trousers and combat jackets. The hardest part was matching the right men with the right boots.

"It's past noon," Hellmann announced. "When this half-track doesn't return to base, things'll start happening. Let's get out of here."

"What about the bodies?" Ward said.

"Leave them where they are." Hellmann fastened the strap of his GI helmet under his chin and climbed up next to Duval.

"And our own uniforms?" Ward said. "We should burn them."

Hellmann was about to agree when Wrack snapped: "We haven't got time. Hide them."

"There's a large and picturesque dungheap," Legge said. "Or wouldn't that be appropriate?"

"It'll do," Wrack said. "Get on with it."

Hellmann knew he should protest—such a procedure was sloppy—but what the hell, it was time they got moving. O'Mara and Chandra poked the discarded uniforms into the dungheap with forks. As they were finishing, Hellmann turned to Ward.

"Ward, come in front with us. If we run into Americans, you or Duval do the talking."

Erika had gone into one of the sheds to change. She emerged, looking dazed and defenseless in a uniform several sizes too large. She looked at Hellmann and he nodded. She climbed up next to him. The others clambered aboard and Duval fired the engine.

The half-track left the dirt road, heading east along a badly potholed road. Despite the sunshine, the air was cold, and still damp with the morning mist. In the sky, a few clouds were beginning to sail toward the north.

"Not too fast," Hellmann told Duval. "We don't want to attract attention. Where did you put the explosives and grenades?"

"On the rack, with all the junk. There's enough C rations in this crate to feed a company. And cigarettes! Any country able to hand out that many cigarettes can't be defeated."

"I think we've got company," Ward said quietly, his voice barely audible above the roar of the motor and the clatter of the treads. He pointed to a distant black spot in the sky.

"Jesus, if that's a Focke Wulf . . ." Duval said.

The plane disappeared behind a hill and then, a moment later, came right at them out of the sun. Hellmann tensed, then relaxed as he spotted the white stars on the wings and fuselage. The P-51 Mustang roared in low over the half-track, dipping its wings in salute. The men in the turret of the vehicle waved back enthusiastically.

Hellmann took out a small map of the region. "We come to a village four or five kilometers from here. We have no choice but to drive through."

"What if the Americans are there already?" asked Ward.

"We go in just the same. Even if it means shooting our way through."

The half-track passed clearings where logs stood

piled in neat stacks, and meadows in which no cattle grazed.

"I saw somebody move on that bridge ahead," Duval said.

"Just keep going."

"Okay, Captain. Hang on."

They rounded a bend at forty-five miles an hour—top speed for the half-track. The men in the rear kept low as the stone parapet of the bridge drew closer. In the cab, Hellmann braced himself to keep his balance as the nine-ton vehicle skidded onto the wooden floor of the bridge, with only a two-foot clearance on either side.

A coal-scuttle helmet appeared over the far end of the parapet. Duval ducked, gripping the steering wheel. Bullets spattered against the cab door. Ward swore, put his hand to his left ear, and brought it back covered with blood.

Rifle and machine-pistol rounds whined round the men in the back. Chandra raised his head above the top of the metal shield. Two snipers. Firing from behind trees. Raising himself further, he brought up his Sten. Legge grabbed him, tried to pull him back under cover. The half-track swerved violently as a grenade exploded in the treads. Simultaneously Chandra was flung backward, hit in the chest. Out of control, the half-track plowed into the parapet. The impact brought down a section of steel girder supporting the span. Duval spun the wheel frenziedly, but it was no good. The half-track was stuck.

"Out! Scatter!" Hellmann roared.

He flung an arm round Erika, rolling her out of the cab. He saw Ward and Duval running at a crouch, O'Mara and Legge blazing away with their Stens, then there was an explosion inside his head and he saw no more.

19

The jeep skidded to a halt in the farmyard and Captain Abernathy slowly unfolded his cramped legs. He rolled his head backward, wincing, kneading the nape of his neck. Behind him, Stachek climbed out of the jeep. A thickset lieutenant with a two-day growth of stubble on his chin was walking toward them.

"Got word to you soon as I could," he said, tossing Abernathy a smart salute. "Thought it might interest you."

Abernathy nodded, and turned to look at the line of corpses laid out side by side.

"My people collected their dog tags," the Lieutenant said. "I and R patrol. Left Mühldorf this morning."

"Any idea who did it?"

"Maybe."

The Lieutenant led them toward the dungheap, which his men were turning over with pitchforks and rakes.

"We found German uniforms."

"How many?"

"Six or seven. The boys are looking some more just in case."

Abernathy squatted beside the dung-soaked clothing. Wrinkling his nose, he lifted trousers and anoraks with the aid of a stick.

"On the sleeves," Stachek said. "The Union Jack insignia."

"I see it." Abernathy stood up. "Bastards."

"Something else," the Lieutenant said. "They may have taken themselves a hostage. The neighbors say there was a girl who lived here. We haven't been able to come up with any trace of her."

"Okay, have all those uniforms brought in and cleaned. By the way, what's your name, Lieutenant?"

"Daniels. I and R platoon, Sixteenth Infantry."

"You've done a good job, Daniels. I may be needing you and your people. You'll work out of my HQ for a few days."

"Are we going after these bastards?"

"We sure are." Abernathy walked back to the jeep. Stachek followed.

"They're tough," the Czech said. "And desperate."

Abernathy shrugged.

On that same day, April 28, on the other side of the globe, an American reporter for Reuters cabled London. His dispatch was based largely on what he'd picked up in the corridors and conference halls of United Nations headquarters in San Francisco. One piece of information seemed particularly fascinating to him. It had been passed on to the reporter by the director of the British Information Office, Jack Winocam. Anthony Eden himself was the source. The item consisted of two typewritten lines: "Western Allies Refuse Any Separate Peace and Demand Germany's Unconditional Surrender."

"Separate" was the keynote of the message. It referred to the attempts by Heinrich Himmler, *"der treue Heinrich,"* to pull his own chestnuts out of the fire by removing Hitler from power and uniting the Allies with the SS in a common struggle against the Soviets.

Through an intermediary, his subordinate Walter Schellenberg, Himmler had been in contact with Count Folke Bernadotte, representing the Swedish Red Cross. For weeks there had been personal talks between the two men; now the Reichsführer's maneuvers were going to be exposed in the world press and broadcast over the radio of the Western Allies.

In the center of besieged Berlin, Heinz Lorenz, an assistant to Propaganda Minister Goebbels, was one of the first to pick up the dispatch. He quickly made two copies, then left his listening post in the basement of the Ministry. He cut across the shell-torn square to the concrete maze of the Führerbunker. Three hundred yards away, fighter bombers with Red Star markings were pounding the thin line of defense set up by General Weidling. Presenting his pass to the bunker sentries, Lorenz strode quickly along the main corridor. Five or six tipsy officers were bawling drinking songs. Lorenz descended to the second level, passed the generator rooms and air-purification plant, the main switchboard, the guardroom, and knocked at the door of the map room, where he knew he would find his direct superior, Propaganda Minister Goebbels.

The little, clean-shaven man, with dark circles under his eyes and a haggard face, was talking to Bormann and Walter Hewel of the Foreign Office. He broke off when he saw Lorenz.

Lorenz handed Goebbels a copy of the dispatch.

Goebbels read it quickly and handed it to Bormann. Bormann's eyes lit up.

"What is the source?" he asked Lorenz.

"The United States and Sweden, via the BBC. The Führer himself asked me to bring him any foreign news that might be important."

Bormann moved toward the door, taking the dispatch with him. He opened it a crack and whispered something to Heinz Linge, Hitler's manservant. Linge took the document and went directly to Hitler's private suite. Hewel and Lorenz left. Goebbels and Bormann were alone. Goebbels was scrawling notes in the margin of a recent copy of his Berlin newspaper, *Panzerbär*, the Armored Bear.

"Well?" Bormann said.

Before Goebbels could reply the door of the map room was flung open. Hitler stood, framed in the doorway, his left arm trembling uncontrollably, his skin purple with anger.

"Another betrayal! At the highest level. At least that fat clown Göring had the decency to ask my permission to enter into negotiations. But Heinrich!"

He staggered toward the table and put both hands on it to support himself.

"He must be arrested," Bormann said smoothly.

"Naturally," Hitler barked. "He's behind a plot of the SS leaders. The upper echelon is rotten to the core. Himmler must be arrested and shot. Where is he? Where's he hiding?"

"Reports from my agents put him in Plön, in north Schleswig-Holstein," Bormann said.

"Send von Greim there. He is faithful and courageous. He will arrest the traitor himself." Then he seemed to remember something. "Fegelein! Where's Fegelein? Bring him here. He must be interrogated immediately. What news is there of Göring?"

"None at the moment," Bormann said. "But he won't escape, my Führer."

"Time," Hitler said. "I need time. A few weeks . . . even a few days . . . I could turn the situation around . . . First Göring . . . now Himmler . . . there's no other way . . . no other way . . ."

"I have confidence, my Führer," said Bormann. "I don't know if von Greim will manage to arrest the Reichsführer, but Göring . . . Göring will be executed according to your orders."

It was a fine hunt. It brought back memories to Wrack. He was a hunter first and foremost; he had always been a hunter. A man hunter.

He had never known his father, but he remembered his mother quite well. "The Beautiful Elfriede," as she was called. Under their breath the neighbors would say, "That beautiful whore Elfriede." And the boys at the elementary school in Charlottenburg repeated it. They didn't say it under their breath.

That was when Wrack began hunting. He would bide

his time for days, sometimes weeks, stalking his prey, waiting for the right moment. Then he would get even with the boys who had insulted his mother. He would use his physical strength as well as his cunning. Invariably the form of his revenge was cruel.

Very early he joined the Party. For him, the Party represented a second family; Elfriede Wrack had been stabbed to death by one of her clients in a cheap Berlin hotel.

The Party offered other advantages: it protected you; it guaranteed you immunity however much violence you used.

And Andreas Wrack loved violence. For its own sake.

In Yugoslavia, assigned to the Wehrmacht's Seventh Mountain Division, he made violence a way of life in the battle against Tito's partisans. He had admired the methods used by the Chetniks. But later he saw that the Chetniks were soft compared to the savage horde recruited and led by Oskar Dirlewanger.

During the weeks he spent with Dirlewanger's unit, Wrack was fascinated by the atmosphere of brutality that reigned permanently among the dregs of German prisons, Ukrainian deserters from the Red Army, and political prisoners recruited in concentration camps, whom Dirlewanger had press-ganged.

Eliminate the enemy at any cost. That was the motto of the Sonderkommando. An excellent motto.

Wrack moved forward cautiously through the bushes, crouching. To his left, O'Mara followed suit. An interesting man, O'Mara. A real killing machine. Dirlewanger would have snapped him up. He would have fitted into the Sonderkommando like a pea in a pod.

Very carefully, Wrack parted the branches in front of

him. Two boys were standing in a clearing, arguing in tense whispers.

The half-track had been ambushed by Hitlerjugend—fourteen-year-old kids in oversized uniforms, armed with looted machine pistols and grenades. Incredible.

Wrack gestured at O'Mara.

The Irishman moved forward, crawling expertly, making not a sound.

The two boys sensed his presence too late. They turned simultaneously, but O'Mara was already up, leveling his Sten at them.

They were paralyzed.

Wrack got to his feet and strode into the clearing. His gray eyes raked the two boys. To him, at that moment, they were the enemy.

Hellmann opened his eyes. At first he seemed to be looking through a blood-red mist. Then he felt a coolness on his brow. Things began coming into focus. The soft, pudgy face of Legge loomed over him. Legge was bathing his brow with a scrap of torn shirt.

"I wouldn't try to talk yet," Ward said. "Your helmet stopped about a dozen rounds. You're concussed."

Hellmann struggled to sit up. Ward was squatting on the grass. His combat jacket was torn. There was a bloodstain on the left shoulder.

"You're hurt," Hellmann said hoarsely.

"Earlobe nicked. It's nothing. Chandra and Duval weren't so lucky."

Hellmann turned his head painfully. His skull was splitting and he felt dizzy. Chandra's body was lying a few feet away. There was a ghastly hole in his chest. Duval lay nearby, motionless, staring up at the sky, which was darkening. The girl, Erika, was sitting beside him.

"Help me get up," Hellmann rasped.

Legge helped him to his feet.

"What about Wrack and O'Mara?" Hellmann asked.

"They're making a sweep of the area."

"Can Duval be moved?"

"I don't know. I'm not a doctor."

"We've got to move out."

Hellmann glanced at Erika. Her face was half concealed under an oversized helmet. She reminded him of his sister, Beate. The same mixture of shyness and knowingness.

He turned back to Ward. "Do we know what happened?"

Ward laughed, a short, harsh laugh. "You won't believe it—it was a couple of Hitlerjugend."

A dry stick cracked in the underbrush nearby and O'Mara and Wrack appeared. They both looked pleased with themselves.

"Well?" Ward said.

Wrack smiled. "We caught the little bastards."

For a moment Hellmann did not understand. Then he did. His voice was a croak.

"You killed them?"

"Naturally."

Hellmann looked at the others. They showed no emotion, except Erika. She was staring at Wrack, as a child stares at a snake.

"There is something else." Wrack sat down on the grass. "There's a small castle, right in the center of the forest. We got fairly close. We heard motors."

"Americans?" Ward asked.

"I doubt it. If the Americans had come through ahead of us we wouldn't have been ambushed by Germans."

"Do we go into the village? Duval needs attention," Ward said.

"Too risky," Wrack replied, checking the magazine of his Schmeisser. "Those boys were almost certainly local. . . . And we need vehicles. We're running out of time. You agree, Hellmann?"

"I suppose so," Hellmann said. "But we can't leave Duval to die here. Make a stretcher."

Legge and O'Mara improvised a litter from two saplings and a strip of tarpaulin. Duval groaned when they lifted him onto it.

"The detonators and explosives are still in the half-track," Ward said.

"We'll have to leave them," Hellmann said. "Let's move."

They set off down the forest track in single file, Wrack leading, Hellmann bringing up the rear. The girl hung back, until she was walking beside Hellmann.

"Is he French—Duval?" she said quietly, as if she didn't wish to be overheard.

"French Canadian."

"What's he doing with you?"

Hellmann saw no reason not to tell her.

"He was fighting in a Canadian unit. He was captured during the raid on Dieppe."

"I remember that."

"He was seriously wounded. In hospital, he was approached by . . . certain people. Duval hates Communism. He's fanatical about it. These people persuaded him that if he wanted to fight the Reds he should fight with

Germany." He shrugged. "I suppose he sees some logic in it."

"He's going to die, isn't he?"

"I don't know."

"My father was killed fighting the Russians. Some little place near Smolensk. They couldn't find enough of his body to give him a proper burial."

"I'm sorry."

"I cried. But then I told myself that he'd died in uniform, fighting for his country."

"That's true."

She looked directly at him. "No it isn't. He died for nothing." She touched his arm. "You're a soldier. A real soldier. Like he was. Let me go. It's getting dark. I can slip away. Please. I'm no use to you."

Hellmann shook his head. "I'm sorry. I'd do it if I could. But for your own protection you must stay with us. If you tried to escape Wrack would kill you. I might not be able to stop him."

They walked on in silence. Then Erika said: "I haven't thanked you. For what you did."

"Are you all right now?"

"I'm sore."

Hellmann was astonished to hear her laugh lightly. "I can hardly sit down."

Wrack was signaling for them to slow down. Before moving forward, Hellmann whispered: "Stay close to me. You'll be all right."

They were at the edge of a dense thicket. A few yards ahead rose the massive walls of the castle, which were pierced in places by narrow windows, in a few of which light showed. The racket of a motorcycle engine shattered the silence.

Legge and O'Mara lowered Duval, unconscious now, to the ground.

"I want to take a closer look," Hellmann whispered.

They moved through the underbrush in a wide circle round the castle. Hellmann could make out only Ward and Wrack, close to his right; night had fallen. Suddenly searchlights sprang on, bathing the courtyard of the castle in yellow light. Two trucks were revving up. Over the noise of the motors, they could hear women laughing. A door opened and a dozen girls emerged, escorted by soldiers.

"My God," Hellmann whispered. "Every bloody one of them is pregnant!"

The soldiers were handing the girls into the backs of the trucks. There was a loud exchange of ribald farewells and kisses. Then the trucks backed up, turned out of the court, and moved away down the forest road.

"What the hell's going on?" Hellmann asked.

Wrack shrugged.

Ward looked away, then, as if speaking to himself, said: "Lebensborn."

"Lebensborn?"

"An organization the Reich can be proud of," Ward said dryly. "The means towards Himmler's publicly stated aim that Germany should be peopled by a hundred and twenty million pure Nordics. We're looking at a breeding factory."

"Whatever it is, whoever they are, they're Germans," said Hellmann. "They can take care of Duval and give us a replacement vehicle."

"I don't like it," Wrack said.

"Have you got a better idea?" Hellmann was deliberately curt.

"Christ!" Ward's voice cracked.

Figures were moving toward the castle. Legge and O'Mara. Carrying Duval. Behind them, Erika. Herding them, with guns leveled, five soldiers and a noncom.

The little column trudged up a stone staircase and vanished into the castle. One soldier remained outside, to stand guard under the walls. His young face was illuminated for a second as he lit a cigarette.

"We've got to get them out of there," Wrack breathed. "Or the whole operation goes down the drain."

"Damn," Hellmann said. "I should have realized there'd be patrols out. You're right. We've got to get them out. We'll have to speak to the senior officer."

"And tell him what?" There was a sneer in Wrack's voice. "Englishmen and Germans in American uniforms. It'd take a week to sort it out. And we haven't got a week."

"What the hell else can we do?"

"Bring about their release."

"We can't attack a castle—start killing our own people."

"Captain Hellmann, you got us into this mess," Ward said.

Hellmann saw that he was trapped. "How do we get in?" he said.

"Leave that to me." Wrack sounded confident, elated. Without another word he slipped away and began to move stealthily toward the castle.

Ward and Hellmann saw him emerge from the undergrowth to their left. He'd removed his GI field jacket and was dressed only in his boots, trousers, and shirt. Unbelievably, he started singing.

". . . *Marschieren mit uns in ihrem Geiste mit!*"

He staggered, as if drunk.

The sentry dropped his cigarette and moved toward

Wrack, unslinging his rifle. Wrack planted his feet wide apart and bawled: *"Du! Komm schnell!"*

The young sentry gaped at the drunken officer. It wasn't a face he recognized. He moved closer, summoning up the courage to challenge the man. Officers in their cups had to be handled with kid gloves.

"Excuse me, sir . . ." he began.

He never finished the sentence. The blade of Wrack's SS dagger flashed in the glare of the searchlights. The sentry staggered, fell, lay still. Wrack dragged the body into cover, then signaled to Ward and Hellmann.

"And an actor too," Ward said.

Wrack grunted, took the Schmeisser that Hellmann handed him.

"Did you have to kill him?" Hellmann said.

Wrack ignored the question. "Let's get a move on."

They climbed the stone stairs in single file and halted before an iron studded oak door. Wrack pushed it open and they entered a shadowy hallway. Muffled voices came from somewhere within the building.

"Right," Hellmann whispered. "We'll split up. Wrack, you and Ward go that way." He jerked his chin at a spiral staircase. "I'll look upstairs. Work fast—they may decide to relieve that sentry."

He snapped his safety off and started up the stairs. Five years of combat and he was about to slaughter fellow Germans. For what? For the Führer? No. For his own survival.

Survive, Erika told herself, that's all that matters. To survive.

In spite of the heat from the gigantic fire roaring in the hearth, she shivered. Someone handed her a glass brimming with champagne. Fingers seized her chin and pushed the rim of the glass against her lips. She looked up at the young German officer and tried to swallow the wine, but half of it slopped over her chin and ran down her throat.

The Untersturmführer—he might have been twenty-two or twenty-three—had a vacant look in his eyes. Under his prematurely white hair his narrow face was crisscrossed with scars.

Dieter Mohr represented a miracle of modern surgery. Serving in an armored division, he had been grievously wounded in the battle of Kursk. For months his life had hung in the balance. A platinum plate had replaced a part of his skull and the reconstruction of his face had required a three-month effort by a team of Dresden surgeons. They had restored Mohr's face—but they could do nothing about his mind. He was a psychopath. His commanding officer knew it, but Mohr had powerful friends in the Party and instead of being locked up in an asylum he had been posted to an isolated castle deep in Bavaria.

"Go on, drink," Mohr said with a chilling smile. "It's the finest champagne from France. You'll see, we have everything. Name it and we'll get it for you."

He indicated the table laden with dirty dishes. "Fruit, vegetables, the best meat, and real coffee—none of that ersatz. There's English tea. We have thirty kilos of caviar in the cellar."

Erika tried to smile—and failed. Drunken soldiers were gorging themselves. On the walls were framed photographs of young, buxom women.

"Our regional breast-feeding champions," Mohr said, following her gaze. "Of course, they can't touch the all-Reich champions, but they've scored fairly high. Louise, there, she delivered 17,211 grams of milk. Reichsführer Himmler wrote her a personal letter of congratulation. Here, drink up."

He handed her another glass, so clumsily that this time most of the champagne splashed onto the parquet floor.

"I'm not thirsty," she mumbled. "Listen, I'm a German, a good German. Just like you. I was a prisoner of those men . . . the ones you captured in the woods. . . . They killed my mother. . . ."

"You men over there—*shut up!*" Mohr shouted. He bent over Erika, staring into her eyes.

"Do you have any idea who those men are? You don't? The villagers call them 'Zuchtbullen,' breeding bulls. Erich!"

Swaying drunkenly, a young soldier came up to Mohr.

"Kindly explain your work to this young lady."

"Certainly, Herr Untersturmführer. I assure the continuity of the race. I make babies . . . for the Führer and the Reich."

"Great work, Fraulein," Mohr said. Then: "Rolf! Martin! Rudi! Horst! Over here!"

He fingered the cloth of Erika's jacket. "Unfortunately," he said, "the only pleasure possible for me is to observe the pleasure of others." His hand darted to her throat without warning. She was paralyzed. Helpless.

"Take her, boys," Mohr said. "One at a time, all together—as you like."

"The situation," Legge said, "calls for philosophy."

He was sitting on the earth floor of the castle cellar, his back against the clammy stone wall. He unlaced his boots to ease his throbbing ankles. A slim beam of moonlight, filtering through an air hole high up in the wall, was the only source of light. The stench of human excrement was overpowering. O'Mara, squatting a few feet away, grunted.

"Do I take that to mean you agree?"

O'Mara didn't answer. He got to his feet and felt his way toward the third man in the cellar. All he could distinguish, in the almost total darkness, was the faint sheen of a shaven head.

"Christ," O'Mara said. "It stinks. Hey, you. Say something."

O'Mara moved closer to the man. He was huddled in a corner, naked except for ragged cotton trousers, shivering with cold.

"*Nye panimaiou*," he croaked.

"Well, well. Would you credit it, now? A Russki."

He felt in his pocket and brought out a bar of K-ration chocolate. He handed it to the Russian. The man hesitated, then snatched the chocolate. He uttered little moans as he gnawed at it. Obviously he was starving.

"*Spasibo, spasibo, spasibo*," he crooned over and over again.

"That's all right, Ivan," O'Mara said. "I like you Russkis. Killed enough to grow fond of you."

He moved away, back toward Legge.

"I'm glad to see you're still cheerful. The irrepressible Irish," Legge said.

"I've got a lifeline on my hand as long as a donkey's cock. I had my palm read by a gypsy at the Cork fair. My time's not yet. Not by a long way."

"I envy your faith in the occult. You think the bold Captain Ward will get us out?"

"Not Ward. Wrack. Wrack'll get us out. He needs us."

"A very alarming young man. But I take your point. He's effective."

"He's bloody brilliant."

O'Mara turned to the Russian. "*Iddee suda*," he said; then, to Legge, "Picked up the Russki blarney on the Eastern Front."

"War—the great educator," Legge said.

"*Iddee suda*," O'Mara repeated.

Very slowly and painfully, the Russian got to his feet. He walked unsteadily toward the Irishman, supporting himself against the wall. His body was emaciated.

O'Mara shrugged out of his combat jacket and handed it to the Russian. The Russian took it, put it on awkwardly, muttering, "*Spasibo, spasibo, spasibo . . .*"

"You're a rum cove, O'Mara. A very rum cove," Legge said.

"The poor bastard's dying of the cold."

"You asked for political asylum in Germany, didn't you?"

After a moment O'Mara said: "I've been at war with the British since I was a kid of four. They killed my father and his three brothers."

"You got what you wanted in the end. An independent republic."

O'Mara laughed. "Is that what they teach you at Eton and Harrow? There are still six counties of Ireland under British rule. And so long as they stay under British rule, so long Sean O'Mara is at war. And what about you, Legge? What are you in it for?"

"The good of my health," Legge said.

21

SS Obergruppenführer Hermann Fegelein, cavalry man and show-jumping champion, had kept his slender, muscular physique. His custom-tailored uniform bore no insignia of rank, yet he maintained the same parade-ground bearing as he had, three years before, when he'd commanded a division on the Ukrainian Front.

Fegelein was Eva Braun's brother-in-law. It was a relationship that had once been extremely valuable, as had his position as Himmler's representative in the bunker. Now that very position seemed to be the reason he was being interrogated by two plainclothesmen from the Berlin Gestapo. The older one, a slender man with prominent ears, was asking questions in a calm, almost disembodied voice. The other was hammering every word spoken onto a typewriter.

"Schellenberg," Fegelein said. "It all started with Schellenberg. His first attempt at negotiations with the American Hewitt in Stockholm was made in defiance of the Reichsführer."

"What was Himmler's reaction?"

"Violent, believe me."

"And yet the Reichsführer changed his mind about that decision. Other contacts were made."

"Yes." He couldn't deny it. He was sweating. He would have to be very clever this time—incriminate Himmler while denying his own responsibility.

"Most of the contacts were made in Switzerland," he went on. "Dr. Langbehn met Allied representatives in Bern in late 1944, during Operation Watch on the Rhine."

"Very interesting. That's something else we knew nothing about. Wasn't there also something about Jews being ransomed?"

"That happened two months ago, in February. A trainload of Jews 'authorized to emigrate' was exchanged for five million Swiss francs, but there was never a second exchange. Nevertheless, I think it safe to say that the Reichsführer had promised to leave the concentration camps intact on the arrival of Allied troops whereas the official orders called for executing or evacuating the prisoners from those camps."

The Gestapo man nodded. He remained lost in thought for a moment. His assistant gathered up the typewritten sheets and handed them to him before packing up his machine.

"Wait here," the Gestapo man ordered as he left the room followed by his assistant.

Alone in the room, Fegelein heaved a sigh and held his head in his hands. As time passed, he began to hope. Abruptly, the door opened. Colonel Högl appeared. Armed men behind him took up positions in the corridor.

"Högl," Fegelein said, "were you able to speak to my sister-in-law?"

The Colonel nodded.

"Well, then?"

"She refused to intercede on your behalf," the Colonel said abruptly. Then he added in a whisper: "I must obey orders, but I could still do you a favor. Is there anything you'd like me to tell your wife?"

Fegelein stared at him, silent. He rose and left the room, Högl behind him. Walking ahead of the SS Leibstandarte escort, the two men went down a corridor past a deserted mess hall where the remains of a meal still cluttered the tables. They climbed a gloomy stairway.

Outside, in the gardens facing the old Chancellery buildings, the chill night air promised frost in the morning. Intermittent shock waves reverberated in the air and the fires started by the Soviet bombardment lit the sky red.

"Where are you taking me?" Fegelein asked.

Högl did not reply. The escort skirted a mud-filled antitank ditch and halted near a low concrete wall. Fegelein glanced at the Colonel inquiringly, but the man averted his gaze.

"I understand," murmured Fegelein.

Without being told to, Fegelein moved to stand with his back to the wall. Automatically, he smoothed the wrinkles out of his tunic.

"Colonel?"

"Yes?"

"My personal belongings. Would you please have them sent to my family?"

Högl nodded and stepped back a pace. The SS Leibstandarte men were already lined up, their weapons trained on the Obergruppenführer.

Fegelein shouted suddenly: "I never conspired against the Führer . . ."

Six shots rang out. Fegelein spun and crashed onto the gravel. Högl walked forward and gave him the *coup de grâce*.

22

Hellmann reached the second floor of the castle. He stopped and stood listening to the sounds from the floor below. Laughter. Snatches of song. What the hell were they celebrating? The end of the war?

He hugged the wall until he reached the first door. Easing it open, he looked into a deserted storeroom. He was closing the door again when he heard a scream. Cold sweat trickled down his back. It was impossible that a human being could scream like that.

He started to run down the corridor. Raised voices filtered through one of the doors, the door through which the scream had come.

"Imbecile, Kurt!"

"Doctor . . ."

"*Dummkopf!* How many times have I told you to double those restraining belts with patients of this kind?"

Cautiously, Hellmann turned the knob and pushed open the door a crack. He looked in. The stark white light of the operating theater made him blink. On a marble-topped table lay the body of a man covered with a soiled sheet. A small man in a white medical coat stood beside the table.

"I've told you again and again, Kurt . . ." he was

saying petulantly. He broke off abruptly, gaping at Hellmann, who advanced into the room, Schmeisser leveled.

"Who . . . who are you?"

He wore thick gold-rimmed glasses. His eyelids fluttered nervously. His assistant opened his mouth as if to speak, then closed it.

Hellmann walked over to the operating table. He lifted a corner of the sheet. Duval had been trepanned. Alive.

"He was dying anyway," the doctor said. "Who are you?"

"A German."

The doctor was visibly relieved. "You have no business being in this part of the castle," he said testily. "We are conducting extremely important research here . . . at the request of Reichsführer Himmler himself."

"What kind of research?"

"On the subject of sleep. We are trying to eliminate certain cells from the brainstem, thereby blocking the interaction of the cortex with the cerebellum. This serves to negate the effects of the hypothalamus."

"For what conceivable purpose are you doing that?"

"The elimination of sleep, of course. Can you imagine an army that marches twenty-four hours a day—nonstop? No fatigue. No need to sleep. Such an army would be invincible!"

Hellmann remembered what Chandra had said about German research into the racial origins of the Nordic people. He had never really believed it. There was a row of glass jars on a shelf level with his eyes. They contained fetuses preserved in formaldehyde. Fetuses with their legs drawn up, smiling serenely. Further on, male genitals, dozens of them.

"Do you call this—science?" Hellmann asked quietly. Something in his face alarmed the doctor.

"Who are you? What are you doing in American uniform?"

Hellmann was looking down at Duval. His face had frozen in a mask of terror, eyes bulging. His right arm had broken the restraining belt like a bit of rotten string, but his heart had been unable to stand the pain.

"Explain yourself," the doctor was saying.

"Certainly," Hellmann said.

"Shut up a moment, will you?" O'Mara hissed. "There's someone coming."

Legge listened. There were thuds—footsteps? it was impossible to tell—coming from the other side of the door.

O'Mara flattened himself against the wall, to the left of the door.

"You haven't got a chance," Legge hissed.

"Get on the other side, you pansy bastard."

"O'Mara . . ."

"Move, God damn you. Take 'em as they come in."

Legge moved. Reluctantly. It wasn't that he didn't think he was as capable as O'Mara of killing any man who came through the door; it was simply that he regarded the action as premature. Too many unknown factors.

Legge and O'Mara waited, tense. The Russian stared at them. He didn't understand what they were doing.

"O'Mara? Legge?"

Ward's clipped voice was faint but unmistakable.

"In here," O'Mara yelled.

They heard the rattle of keys in the lock, then the door swung open.

Ward was standing in the dimly lit passage. Behind him, Wrack was kneeling beside the body of a young guard, cleaning his dagger on the tunic of the man he had just killed.

"Where's Hellmann?" O'Mara said, stepping out of the cellar and taking the machine pistol Ward was offering him.

"Upstairs."

Legge came out, closely followed by the Russian. The Russian was blinking almost comically.

"What in God's name is that?" Ward said.

"A Russian," O'Mara said.

"What's he doing here?"

"I've no idea at all."

Wrack was eyeing the Russian.

"*Tye!*" he said suddenly. "*Kak tibya zavoot?*"

The Russian gaped, then replied eagerly: "Grigor Pavelovich Cherkov."

"*Putchemoo tye zdyes?*" What are you doing here?

"*Ya nye znayoo*," answered the Russian with a shrug.

"*Gdye tye bil rano?*" Wrack asked. Where were you before?

"*V Chemnitz.*"

"What do we do with him?" O'Mara asked.

"He comes with us," Ward said.

At the end of the corridor was a small guardroom with bunk beds, a long table, and half a dozen chairs. A young guard, clad only in his underwear, lay on a lower bunk, his throat cut from ear to ear.

"What a busy night you're having, Lieutenant Wrack," Legge said.

The Russian picked up a rifle that had been slung over a bedpost, and checked it professionally. Wrack scowled, but Ward said, "We can use another man."

112

Wrack scouted to the far end of the next corridor. "All right," he called. "It's clear ahead."

"What about Hellmann?" O'Mara asked again.

"He'll meet us," said Ward, snapping off the safety from his Sten. "We'll wait near the stairs."

In single file they headed for the hall. They could hear whoops and whistles, like men cheering on a football team.

"What are we waiting for?" Wrack muttered, jerking his head in the direction of the stairs. "At any moment they may check the sentries."

"We wait," snapped Ward. "Hellmann will be here."

"Certainly," Hellmann repeated.

He squeezed the trigger of the Schmeisser, sending a three-round burst into the doctor's belly. Unhurriedly, he trained the muzzle on the assistant. He squeezed again. The second burst flung the man into the shelves of jars, which shattered, spattering their contents over him as he died.

Hellmann let out his breath in a long sigh. Then he moved swiftly to the door. All hell was about to break loose.

He came to the stairs and paused. Why not get out now? He'd seen enough, done enough. Nothing mattered anymore except his own survival.

But the girl. Erika.

She means nothing to me, he told himself. I mean nothing to her. She has every reason to hate me. I led the men who turned her home into a slaughterhouse. But still, she deserves a chance to survive. I owe her that.

At the first burst of gunfire, Ward, Wrack, O'Mara, and Legge had frozen. At the second, Ward had said: "Hellmann! That's Hellmann."

Seconds trickled by, then there were panicky yells and three Germans ran across the hall. Wrack wheeled and fired from the hip. Two of the Germans hit the flagstones. The third managed to reach the door of the dining hall. A single rifle shot cut him down. The Russian lowered his weapon, grinning.

Hellmann appeared, his face ashen but his manner cool.

"Duval?" Ward snapped.

"Dead."

"Erika?" Hellmann said.

"She must be in there—in the dining hall."

"Right. Let's go."

"Wait," Wrack said.

"I'm not arguing, Wrack."

The gunfire in the hall had finally alerted Mohr to the danger. But too late.

As he drew his Luger, the door was kicked open and machine-gun fire flailed across the room. It caught Mohr, picked him up, and flung him against the wall.

Hellmann advanced into the room, firing short bursts. Years of training, years of combat, enabled him to assess the situation instantly. Erika: lying on her back near the fire. One man, naked, standing over her. Group of three to the left. Diving for their guns. Two more on the right. Seventh man lying by the wall. Eighth man, running.

He picked off the naked man near Erika first. He heard reports behind him. Ward. The running man went down. He fired two bursts at the group of three. O'Mara was by his side, aiming coolly at the men on the right.

Ward and O'Mara. Professionals.

Instinct made him flick his eyes to the white-haired

man lying by the wall. He swung his Schmeisser. But he was seconds too late. Mohr's Luger spat twice before Hellmann's fire riddled his body.

Ward's legs buckled. Hellmann caught him as he fell, lowered him gently to the floor as O'Mara, his eyes wild, fired burst after burst, in a frenzy.

And then there was silence.

Hellmann was kneeling by Ward. Mohr's bullets had hit him in the spine. It was hopeless.

Ward's eyes were open.

"Ward," Hellmann began.

Ward shook his head. Hellmann thought he was trying to smile. His lips moved. Hellmann bent closer to catch his words.

Legge was squatting by them. He took Ward's wrist, felt for his pulse.

Ward was trying to say something with his eyes, trying to communicate. It went on for what seemed like an hour, but was only a minute. Then the light went out of his eyes and Legge released Ward's wrist.

"Did you hear what he said?" Legge asked. Hellmann stared at him. Legge's face was haggard; it was a different Legge, suddenly.

"Yes," Hellmann said. "Yes, I think so. I think he said: 'I've wanted this for a long time.'"

Legge nodded. "That sounds . . . right," he said.

23

"My hand ain't so great," Sergeant DiSalvo said, "but I think I'll raise you five anyway."

He counted the dollar bills stacked before him and laid them out in a neat line on the desk. Lieutenant Daniels smiled to himself and threw in his cards. He'd met sharps like DiSalvo before. Abernathy drew on one of DiSalvo's foul cigars and shook his head. Only Greenbaum, the fat Signal Corps PFC, matched the five-dollar raise.

DiSalvo turned over his cards. Three aces.

"And you drew four cards," Greenbaum said disgustedly, exposing three queens.

DiSalvo laughed and raked in the pot.

Sitting alone at the far end of the room, Stachek dozed, his back against the wall. He'd had a long, disappointing day. The Americans were incompetent fools. A whole day wasted. Nothing done. The war would be over before he had a chance to get back at Wrack. He opened his eyes as he heard the sound of footsteps. The door of the classroom opened abruptly and an infantry major appeared. Abernathy, Daniels, Greenbaum, and DiSalvo got to their feet casually, and saluted Major Fen-

116

ner carelessly. Abernathy handed Fenner a half-empty bottle of Haig and Haig.

"You drag me all the way here for a slug of scotch, Ab?" the Major said. "Right this minute, I should be at a party at the General's. Instead, I do twenty miles in a jeep that isn't winterized, with a half-witted driver and two mental-defective privates. This better be something serious."

"It is," Abernathy said.

"You haven't found that damned Alpine Fortress of theirs again, have you?"

Abernathy grinned. "No, sir."

"Shame. I've got Patch, Patton, Eisenhower, *and* Montgomery breathing down my neck for intelligence on that lousy redoubt."

Abernathy summoned Stachek. "I want you to hear what our friend here has to say. He speaks German, so I'll translate."

The Major looked at the Czech suspiciously.

"The night before last," Stachek said, "Hitler and Bormann condemned Göring to death. Two Germans left Berlin to carry out the order. In Brno, they picked up five British Waffen SS. These seven men are in the area right now."

Abernathy translated.

"British SS?" the Major queried. "Sounds like a crock of shit to me. Ab?"

"It's no baloney, Major. No, Sir, you can check it yourself. Look"—he pointed to the uniforms laid out on the chair—"these British Corps people got themselves some new uniforms by a very simple process—they ambushed one of our I and R patrols at the Kiesel farm."

"Sons of bitches," murmured the Major.

117

"If my memory serves correctly, Major, Göring's considered the third most wanted war criminal. An arrest could mean promotions."

"Yeah." The Major stroked his chin. "But there's a hitch."

"What's that?"

"Göring isn't in Mauterndorf anymore. We just got the news. He's hiding out near Zell-am-See. Exactly where, we don't know, but we'll find out pretty soon. Up to now there hasn't been any special rush, but if this business about British SS is true, we've got to stop them before they screw it up. You got any thoughts?"

Abernathy strode over to the wall map of the area.

"Here's the Kiesel farm. Here—Mauterndorf. In my opinion, those British Corps bozos went that way. They may be already in Mauterndorf. They could be holed up somewhere. Now, there's a village right here. Daniels can take his scouts there tonight and go in at dawn. If he doesn't get 'em, he might pick up their tracks."

The Major pondered a moment. Finally he said: "Okay, Ab. We'll do it your way."

"We'll get 'em, sir."

"Yeah. You get 'em. And get 'em good."

24

It was a bedroom. A feminine sort of room, with bright chintzes and flowered wallpaper. Hellmann wondered who the hell had occupied it.

Erika was sitting in front of an ornate cherrywood and ormolu dressing table. She had found a frock from somewhere—a simple, expensive-looking frock that suited her. She was brushing her hair.

She seemed to be utterly calm, in control of herself. Incredible, considering that she'd been raped at least five times, not half an hour ago.

"Are you all right?" Hellmann said. He felt curiously shy and ill at ease. The girl was so damned self-possessed suddenly.

"Look. Do you want something? Brandy? Whiskey? There's everything here."

She shook her head. "I'm fine. Really."

"Fine?"

She turned. Her face was hard, set. "What do you expect? Tears? Hysteria? I'm alive."

"Yes, but . . ."

"I wasn't innocent—before all this started. I'd seen people die. I'd had men. Perhaps you don't know what life has been like in Germany for civilians."

"Not like it's been for you in the last twenty-four hours."

"Oh yes," she said. "The same. Only more so. Don't waste your sympathy on me, Captain. I don't want that. I just want to get out of this alive."

"Of course. You could just disappear."

"I could. But like you said before, what about Wrack? And I don't know what's going on out there."

"You mean you now want to stay with us?"

"I want to stay with you. You said you'd protect me. I believe you. What are you going to do?"

"I don't know."

"Why don't we get away together? I'd feel safe with you. You don't believe in your mission."

She stood up and walked over to him.

"Killing Göring. It's mad. What's the point of it? The war's nearly over. Are you a Party member?"

Hellmann smiled. "No."

"Then why go on? It's pointless. It's crazy."

"I know. I knew that from the start. I received my orders directly from Hitler. In his study in the Führerbunker. He's a demented old man. A cripple, in body and mind. Believe me, I have no illusions left. But—I don't know. I've spent five years of my life fighting. For a lost cause, I suppose. Or the wrong cause. Perhaps I see this mission as a trial, a sort of purging."

"I don't understand. We could get out of here. Together. Now."

She put a hand on his arm. *"Please,"* she said.

"Maybe. I'll see what's happening. Stay here. Lock the door. Don't let anyone in. Here." He drew his Schmeisser and gave it to her.

He left the room determined to get out. To hell with

Wrack. He'd kill him if necessary. To hell with all of them. The girl was right. It was pointless to go on.

In the dining hall, O'Mara, Legge, and the Russian were guzzling food. There was no sign of Wrack.

Ward's body lay where it had fallen, covered with a tablecloth stained with wine and blood. The other corpses also lay where they had fallen. Hellmann thought there was something macabre in the spectacle of O'Mara and Legge eating and drinking in that charnel house.

"How's the young lady?" Legge said.

He seemed to have recovered his usual spirits.

"All right."

"The poor dear. All those *men*. Perhaps she enjoyed it. They say women do, you know."

O'Mara grinned. Then he shook his head. "Fuckin' shame, Ward stopping one."

"Hypocrisy," Legge said. "The national sport of Ireland. You hated Ward's guts."

O'Mara shrugged. "Only as a matter of principle. He was one hell of a man. You know what he said to me once? 'You can have the whole of Ireland tomorrow, O'Mara,' he said. 'You're welcome to it. *My* money's in Switzerland.' Yes"—he chuckled—"one hell of a man."

"Where's Wrack?" Hellmann said.

"Conducting a room-by-room search of the place. Such a dedicated officer," Legge said.

Hellmann walked across the hall and up the main stairs. There was no sign of Wrack on the first floor. He mounted to the next floor. The first room he entered was dominated by a bust of Adolf Hitler. There were shelves loaded with silver cups, sporting trophies. He went back into the corridor. He heard a sound from the next room. The door was open a crack. He pushed it gently.

121

Wrack was sitting on a stool. He was wearing a headset and holding a transmitter on his right knee. Wrack turned slowly, removing the headset and placing the transmitter on a table.

"Any news?" Hellmann asked.

"The Americans are still being held along the Elbe. Berlin is completely encircled and the Russians are pushing into the center of the city. In Czechoslovakia there was an attempted mutiny among Vlasov Ukrainians. They've been deserting in droves since they heard the Red Army was outside Prague."

"What about Bavaria?"

"The advance elements of the U.S. Seventh Army are close to Berchtesgaden. It won't be long before they're here."

"I see. And did you succeed in contacting HQ?"

"Yes," Wrack admitted coolly.

"And?"

Wrack smiled thinly but remained silent.

"Listen, Wrack. We've lost three men. We haven't got a chance of getting to Göring. Even if we had, there's no sense in it. The war's over—and lost."

"I calculated from the start that we'd lose men. We have an excellent chance, Captain Hellmann. As to the other—the outcome of the war is irrelevant. We have been given certain orders. We have no alternative but to carry them out."

"All right. *You* carry them out. Maybe you can persuade O'Mara and Legge to go with you. Or the Russian. But not me. I'm finished."

"I don't think so, Captain," Wrack said. He rose.

"You can try to kill me," Hellmann said wearily, "but it's better than evens that I'll kill you first."

"I don't have to kill you, Hellmann. You will do your duty. Minister Bormann foresaw this, as he foresees every contingency. You have a sister, I believe. Beate? She was taken into custody yesterday, by order of the Führer."

Something inside Hellmann snapped. He lunged at Wrack, sinking his fingers into his throat. Wrack lashed out. His knee pumped, trying to find Hellmann's groin. But at that moment Hellmann could have throttled a thousand Wracks. His fingers sank into Wrack's flesh as if it were dough. Hideous choking noises gurgled in Wrack's throat. His body went slack.

And then Hellmann felt cold metal against his ear and heard O'Mara's voice.

"That's enough. Let him go. Right now."

Slowly, Hellmann released Wrack, who collapsed onto the floor, plucking at his neck, drawing in air with rasping wheezes.

O'Mara stepped back, still covering Hellmann with his Sten.

Wrack was vomiting uncontrollably.

"I hope he doesn't die. For your sake, Captain Hellmann," O'Mara said. "Wrack has something I want. Two thousand pounds and a new identity."

Hellmann laughed—a harsh, bitter laugh. "He'll survive." He addressed Wrack, who was still clutching his throat, but breathing more easily. "We'll start out as soon as you're fit."

He turned and, ignoring O'Mara's gun, walked out.

He ran down the stairs and knocked on Erika's door.

"Who is it?"

"It's all right. It's me."

The door opened and Hellmann went into the bedroom.

"I'm sorry," he said without preamble. "I'm carrying on with the mission. I have no choice." Briefly, he explained. "You can stay here—or just go, right now."

She shook her head. "I'll stay with you."

"I think you'd be better off on your own."

"No. I want to stay with you. Are you sure Wrack isn't bluffing?"

"Oh yes. It rings true. And even if he is—I can't call his bluff, can I? I'm in a trap. I've been in a trap from the moment I entered the Führerbunker."

25

Walter Wagner was sweating with terror. The fifty-year-old municipal bureaucrat had spent his life working in back rooms, obscurely, devotedly, and above all, safely. He was a typical minor official of the Party, with a modest apartment, a modest salary, and modest ambition.

Bormann's summons to the Führerbunker had come like a summons to a firing squad.

Wagner glanced nervously at his silent SS escort. In front of him, Colonel Högl was walking rapidly, never turning round. Wagner wanted to ask him some questions but he simply couldn't summon up the courage. They went down the emergency stairs into the bunker. They passed through an anteroom, then the map room, where a dozen or so junior officers were studying the charts. They halted before the door that led to Hitler's private conference room. Högl knocked three times and Goebbels appeared.

"Ah, Wagner," he said, quite genially. "Thank you, Högl, you may go."

Högl nodded stiffly and moved away, followed by his men. His legs trembling, Walter Wagner entered the holy of holies. Inside his Volkssturm uniform he was sweating.

"Have you brought the papers?" Goebbels rapped out.

"The papers? Oh, yes, of course Herr Reichsminister. The . . . the banns haven't been published yet and I'm still missing—"

"All right, all right," said Goebbels impatiently. "That can all be arranged in due course."

A door opened and Wagner gulped as he saw the Führer in person enter the room. But Hitler's manner seemed to be positively friendly. He thanked Wagner for turning out at such an hour of the night. Behind Hitler were Bormann and Eva Braun. She was wearing a very simple blue dress, without any jewelry.

"Herr Wagner," Hitler said, "I called you here for a marriage—my own marriage. Is there any objection to the banns being concluded orally in the circumstances?"

"None, my Führer," Wagner just managed to reply.

Goebbels was clearing the desk, laying out the forms Wagner had brought. Wagner took up his position opposite Hitler and Eva Braun. Bormann and Goebbels, the witnesses, stood to one side.

Wagner cleared his throat nervously. There was a strict formula to be followed. "Do you solemnly swear," he said, "that you are both of pure Aryan descent?"

"I swear," Hitler's voice was crisp, loud.

"I swear," echoed Eva Braun.

"And neither of you is suffering from any hereditary illness that might preclude this marriage?"

Both of them swore.

When they came to the exchange of signatures and the formalities concerning the parents of the married couple, Hitler hesitated, then left blank the names of his father, Alois Hitler, and his mother, Klara Pölzl. The bride took the pen and signed Eva Braun, then crossed it out and wrote: Eva Hitler, née Braun.

"I now declare you united by the bonds of matrimony," Wagner said. He had regained his composure and was preparing to launch into a congratulatory speech when Hitler thanked him briefly and Goebbels ushered him to the door.

Several people were waiting in Hitler's private sitting room. Magda Goebbels was whispering with the Führer's two secretaries, Frau Christian and Frau Junge. Generals Krebs and Burgdorf were exchanging information about the deteriorating situation in Berlin and its suburbs. Hitler's vegetarian cook, Constanze Manzialy, stood wretchedly alone in a corner.

As Hitler and his wife entered, followed by Goebbels and Bormann, everyone crowded around to congratulate the bride and groom. Hitler shook hands all round and Eva offered her cheek to the women.

"Will you kindly take your glasses," Bormann said.

"We will drink a toast to the health of the newlyweds."

He poured the champagne while Magda Goebbels handed out biscuits and cake.

"Do you remember when I was best man at your wedding, Magda?" Hitler asked.

"That was a tremendous honor—and the most lovely day of my life. We have had other joys, but that day has always seemed the most important day of my life."

"So much has happened since then. So many of our friends have died . . . not to mention the ones who have abandoned me . . . betrayed me along the way . . . Röhm . Hess . . . even Heinrich . . . my faithful Heinrich. Treason, always treason . . . in the upper echelon. Göring."

"*He* will be punished," Bormann said in an attempt to rally Hitler. "That traitor will not escape the Führer's justice."

"No. No."

There was a long silence. They all knew what would come next.

"The great plan of National Socialism is finished," Hitler said. "I represented a doctrine and a vital force. With me gone, the rest is nothing but clay and dust. But I will always remain in the memory of men and in history . . . Frau Junge?"

"Yes, my Führer?"

"Accompany me to my study, if you please."

He moved away, his back bent, his eyes half closed. Frau Junge followed obediently.

Hitler sat under the portrait of Frederick the Great, Frau Junge opposite, her pad on her knee, her pencil in hand. Hitler consulted his typewritten notes. As he began to speak, Frau Junge's pencil flew over the pages.

"I expel Heinrich Himmler and Hermann Göring from the National Socialist Party. In opening negotiations with the enemy and seeking to take power, they committed a crime against the nation and the Führer.

"After my death, Admiral Doenitz will assume the presidency of the Reich, command of the armed forces, and the Ministry of War. His government will comprise: Goebbels as Chancellor; Bormann as Chancellor of the Party; Seyss-Inquart will handle Foreign Affairs; von Krosigk, Finance . . .

"International Jewry, that universal poison, must be fought with every possible means . . ." Hitler's voice droned on and on, with long silences occasionally intervening. At last he got to his feet painfully and signed the papers.

"Now go find Goebbels and Bormann," he told his secretary. "Krebs, and Burgdorf as well. Tell them to report here without delay."

He waited a few minutes in the silence of his study, reading over the terms of his political will. Two discreet knocks were heard and the four men appeared.

"Read this and sign it," Hitler said.

They obeyed without comment. The designation of Doenitz as head of the government was an unwelcome surprise but, with the Führer's eyes on them, none of the men dared betray the slightest disapproval.

"And here is my personal will," said Hitler handing them a second sheaf of papers. "As you can see, Martin, you are my executor. Part of your task involves taking care of my wife's mother and providing any assistance needed by those who served on my staff."

Bormann gave him a little bow.

"Does this mean, my Führer," Goebbels ventured to

ask, "that you're contemplating . . . er . . . the idea of giving up the struggle?"

He had not dared to use the words *ending your life*.

"That's exactly what I'm contemplating," Hitler answered. "Now, gentlemen, you must get some rest. We'll see each other at lunch."

Hitler withdrew almost at once, followed by Krebs and Burgdorf. Goebbels and Bormann remained alone in the study. The Minister of Propaganda collapsed into an armchair.

"It's all over. None of us can survive the Führer's death."

Bormann nodded, his face expressionless.

"I'm going to make my arrangements," Goebbels said.

He left Bormann and went to his own rooms. Bormann, walking rapidly, left the Führer's study and crossed the map room and the main corridor. He went up the stairs to the first level of the bunker. On the way he passed Dr. Stumpfegger, but was so preoccupied that he didn't even look at him. The machine room for the generators and air-conditioners was deserted and he walked through it swiftly. This brought him to the cramped cubbyhole that housed the emergency switchboard. There was only one man there, lying fully clothed on a folding cot. He had a three-day growth of beard and his face was ashen with fatigue.

"Can we still send messages to the outside?" Bormann asked.

"Yes, Herr Minister," the man replied. "But the Russians are less than three hundred meters away."

"I'm well aware of that," Bormann snapped. "Have you received any news from my family?"

The man fumbled through a sheaf of messages. He handed one to Bormann.

BERCHTESGADEN. 29/0403. "BERGMANN" FAMILY IS TO JOIN CONVOY UNDER ESCORT LEAVING FOR SOUTH TYROL. DESTINATION: SILVA (VAL-GARDENA—DOLOMITES). RECORDS AND DOCUMENTS SAFE. HAVE MADE ALL ARRANGEMENTS TO HAVE MARTIN ADOLF BROUGHT FROM STEINACH TO SILVA. VON HUMMEL.

Bormann sighed softly. Excellent. His wife, his sister, and his son Martin Adolf would soon be safe, far from the combat zone. His secret papers, correspondence, and personal notes would be sent to another place, also secret. He could now turn his attention to his own future.

"Nothing else for me?" he asked.

"Wait a minute."

Again the radio operator hunted through the sheaf of messages, and after a moment handed Bormann a scrap of paper with a few words scrawled on it in pencil: "Fenris to Asgard. Three fangs pulled. Mission in difficulty."

Bormann took a moment to absorb Wrack's message and decide what to do about it. He did decide. But first the arrangements for his own family. Second, a message to the twins in regard to Fenris.

"Here's the first message I want you to transmit," he said to the radio operator, handing him a typewritten sheet. "Send it three times, at thirty-second intervals. End the third transmission with a series of four Ns."

When the operator had completed the transmission Bormann handed him a second message.

"New channel?"

"Of course. And repeat this one three times as well."

ASGARD TO JOTUNNHEIM. OPERATION FENRIS CANCELED.
MAKE ALL ARRANGEMENTS FOR RECOVERY AND DISPERSAL.
SANCTION—REPEAT—SANCTION PRIOR TO WITHDRAWAL.
THOR.

26

Hellmann, Wrack, Erika, and Legge walked across the
hall, opened the main door of the castle, and went down
the steps. In the dark, O'Mara was gunning the engine of
a captured English Bedford truck, repainted in Wehrmacht camouflage colors.

"She'll do," he said. "Where's little Ivan?"

"Dead drunk," Legge said. "He found a case of vodka
and . . ."

"We'll leave him then. Fuel?" Hellmann asked.

"Plenty," O'Mara said.

"OK. Let's get on with it. We'll head for the village."

The Bedford puttered slowly out of the courtyard,
crunched over the gravel, then bumped onto the forest
road.

The dirt track brought them out to the main highway.
A fine rain began to fall and O'Mara signaled to Hellmann

to operate the manual windshield wipers.

Fifteen minutes later the first houses of a typical south German village began to appear. It was as if the place had been abandoned. But Hellmann sensed that there were eyes behind the metal shutters; frightened, watchful eyes.

O'Mara turned into the main square and brought the Bedford to a stop under a clump of trees by the bandstand. He switched off the ignition and lights, then climbed out of the cab. Hellmann and Erika followed. Wrack and Legge jumped down over the tailgate. Hellmann hesitated. He glanced at Wrack and the latter nodded in the direction of a two-story building. Gothic lettering on a signboard over the entrance spelled KREUS.

"If we have to wait till morning," Wrack said, "we might as well wait in comfort."

Hellmann nodded. O'Mara and Legge covered him as he marched across the muddy square, up to the massive wooden door of the inn. He knocked twice with the stock of his machine pistol. Nothing happened for two or three minutes, then the door opened a crack. A tiny old man in a flannel dressing gown peered out.

"American? Welcome . . . er . . . What do you want?"

"This is an inn, yes?" Hellmann said in German.

"Yes, sir. But . . . er . . . we're closed," the man stammered.

"I think you'll manage to find rooms for us." Hellmann raised his Schmeisser. The little man stood back as Hellmann strode inside.

"We give only bed and breakfast," the innkeeper whined.

"How many people in the house?" Wrack barked.

"Three . . . no, four," the little man corrected himself.

"My mother and my wife, plus the apprentice who lives in the attic room. And me, of course."

"How many rooms?"

"Six, but because of the war . . ."

"Look," Hellmann said, kindly but firmly, "we want a room each, and something to eat, right away. We won't harm you. At dawn we'll clear out."

Hellmann went to the door and beckoned to the others. He turned back to the innkeeper.

"Tell me," he asked, "are there regular Wehrmacht troops stationed in the village?"

"No, no. Nothing. Just a few boys of the Hitlerjugend, but they're all hiding now."

In virtual silence Hellmann, Erika, Wrack, O'Mara, and Legge ate a meal of ersatz bread, sausage, cheese, and beer in the cold candle-lit dining room. Then they climbed the stairs to the second floor and went to their rooms.

The sight of the eiderdown quilt on his bed made Hellmann want to cry. He had almost forgotten that such things existed. He ripped off his clothes, placed his Schmeisser on the bedside table, switched out the light, and fell into the bed. Within a few seconds he was asleep.

In Crete, during the 1941 campaign, Hellmann had managed to sleep whole nights under massive RAF bombings. It had been the same during the Ardennes counteroffensive in late 1944. The endless columns of German tanks that had ground relentlessly past the small Luxembourg hotel had never disturbed him. But for some reason, in the silence of that Bavarian inn, the slight creak of a floorboard wakened him instantly. He did not move. The gray dawn was beginning to filter through cracks in the shutters and a shadowy figure was moving toward his bed.

"Erika," he whispered.

She didn't answer. He saw that she was slipping out of her dress. A shaft of pale light touched her breasts as she stooped to get into the bed. Then her body, warm, silky-textured, was pressed against his.

He lay very still. She stroked his chest, his belly, and thighs, but he did not respond.

"You'd be better off in Wrack's bed, or even O'Mara's. They're real survivors," he said.

She didn't withdraw her hand. But she rested it lightly on his inner thigh.

"Is that what you think?"

"Isn't it true?"

"Yes. I suppose so. No. I wanted to—as well. Anyway, does it make any difference?"

Did it?

Hellmann was fully awake now. His body was beginning to respond to the presence of a woman in his bed, independently, it seemed, of his mind.

Erika's hand traveled a few inches upward.

She giggled. It was an extraordinarily infectious, intimate sound. It was as if they were old lovers, sharing a private erotic memory.

Hellmann turned to her, seeking her mouth with his own.

"I've wanted to," she whispered, "ever since . . ."

"Ever since when?"

"Ever since we talked in the forest. Walking to the castle."

When it was over—and it was brief, wild, uncontrolled—they lay side by side, Hellmann smoking a cigarette.

"Don't you blame me—at all—for what happened to your mother?" Hellman asked.

134

"Do we have to talk about that?"

"You must blame me."

"I don't. I don't even blame Wrack. Or O'Mara. I suppose if anyone's to blame it's Hitler and Bormann. And who's to blame for Hitler and Bormann? Germany."

"You're a philosopher."

"You mean I'm hard-bitten."

"No."

"I am. I never loved my mother. I didn't even like her. She exploited me. You know all that food and wine you found. I earned most of that. With my body."

Hellmann found himself telling her something he had never told another living soul, as if his mind had been taken over by someone else.

"When I was a boy, in Berlin," he said, "in the depression, I earned money to feed my family by soliciting in the streets. Men. I mean homosexual men."

"Thousands of boys did that in those days."

"I suppose they did."

"Tell me about your family. Tell me about your mother. Is she still alive?"

"I don't really know. She was reported missing. I expect she is."

"Is she a survivor, then?"

"Of a sort. She's a character. She had no money, no education. She married a penniless language teacher. But she never forgot she was a baroness, a member of the noble house of Laupheim. She refused to cook, to clean the house. She would spend all day sewing for some charity started by the Empress Someone-or-Other."

He laughed lightly. "But you know she really loved my father. He used to write things—essays and poems. She couldn't wait for him to become a famous writer, so he could be her social equal. She used to say that art transcends class."

"And your father?"

"He's dead. He was killed in an air raid. I'm glad in a way. He couldn't have stood seeing—what's happened to Germany. He was a devout National Socialist, you see." He laughed again, wryly. "It was about his only fault. He was a very kind, gentle sort of man."

Hellmann suddenly fell silent. He was thinking of Beate, his sister.

"Don't move," O'Mara hissed. "Not a muscle."

Wrack froze.

O'Mara chuckled softly. The SS Lieutenant felt the cold metal of a Sten on his cheek.

"A little advice, Lieutenant," O'Mara said. "Always bolt a door. Locks are that easily picked. Now, get your boots on. Very, very carefully."

Wrack pushed back the blankets. Except for his boots, he was fully clothed.

As he sat on the edge of the bed, struggling to pull his boots on, he calculated the risk of making a dive for his Schmeisser, only a foot or so away on the table. He decided the risk was too great. O'Mara was a formidable man.

"Very good," O'Mara said. "Now, stand up. We're going to take a little walk together, Lieutenant, to the truck. Then we'll take a little drive to that hunting lodge you've mentioned. Then we're going to transact a little business. And then we'll say good-bye."

Wrack's tension relaxed a fraction. Between the room and the truck he'd get his chance.

But by the time they had crept down to the front door, Wrack was not so sure. The Irishman had given him not a shred of a chance.

He stood at precisely the right distance from Wrack as he unbolted the door, but again Wrack saw hope. The truck. O'Mara would have to let him take the wheel. And that would give him all sorts of chances.

He started across the square, O'Mara three paces behind.

The lights seemed to spring from nowhere. Both Wrack and O'Mara were frozen for an instant in their glare as three jeeps roared into the square.

O'Mara hurled Wrack aside and opened fire. Then he grabbed Wrack, yelling: "Back inside!"

Hellmann was out of bed and struggling into his clothes before the echoes of O'Mara's burst had died.

He was forcing on his boots when the window shattered and splinters flew from the shutter. He yelled at Erika to get down. He crawled to the window and raised his head inch by inch.

American jeeps. Three. Air-cooled machine guns. Men running at a crouch, taking up positions. Ringing the house.

O'Mara burst into the room.

"Yanks," he panted. "And that bastard Stachek's with them."

Hellmann ran into the passage. Legge was stumbling out of his room, fighting into his jacket.

"What the hell's going on?"

"Americans. Stachek's with them."

"Christ."

Wrack appeared, cramming a magazine into his Schmeisser.

"A diversion," Hellmann said. "Before they get the layout and establish positions. Out the back, circle, try to grab one of their jeeps."

They heard O'Mara's Sten blazing away in Hellmann's room.

"Brilliant," Wrack said. "And who provides the diversion?"

"I'll do it," Legge said.

Wrack stared at him.

"I said I'd do it," Legge repeated, without a trace of a drawl in his voice. "But for Christ's sake let's get a move on. I'll sortie through the front door. You go out the back."

"Right." Hellmann dashed back into his room. "O'Mara—out the back with the others, Wrack'll explain. Erika. You've got to stay."

"I'm coming with you."

"No—"

"I'm coming with you."

Legge was in a position in the hall, standing by the front door. He had two Stens and four or five grenades. Hellmann pounded down the hall. He was panting hard. "Start in exactly half a minute from when I leave you."

"Half a minute right. Right."

There was no time, but Hellmann had to know.

"Why are you doing this, Legge? It's suicidal."

"You wouldn't understand, my dear," Legge said, with his old drawl.

"Try me."

Legge looked at him quizzically.

"Well," he said, "you see, I'm a National Socialist. I believe that Adolf Hitler was the greatest hope for the future that Europe has known in a thousand years. I

138

believe that his failure is a monumental tragedy. I am quite prepared to die for National Socialism—die with it, I should say. Like Ward, only for different reasons, I have been waiting a long time for this moment."

He smiled at Hellmann's expression. "You see. I told you that you wouldn't understand. Good-bye, my dear. I'll do my best for you." He looked at his watch. "Half a minute."

Hellmann turned. He ran down the passage to the kitchens. Wrack, O'Mara, and the girl were crouching by the back door. Erika was holding Hellmann's Schmeisser.

The blast of a grenade announced that Legge's diversion had begun.

"Go," Hellmann said. "Erika. With me."

In the square the Americans could hardly believe their eyes.

"Jesus, they're coming out the front," Daniels yelled. "Concentrate your fire on the front."

A second grenade detonated in the square. Daniels ducked the blast. Through the smoke he saw a figure zigzagging across the square. He opened fire with his machine pistol.

"Get those fuckin' machine guns on the front."

Another grenade exploded. Daniels saw a second man darting out of the front door, firing from the hip. In fact it was Legge, who had doubled back. He threw a fourth grenade, repeated the maneuver, firing long bursts at the jeep on the far side of the square. He saw two of the gunners spin and fall.

The square was an inferno of machine-gun fire. Legge was hit. Once. Twice. Again. But he was still moving . . . toward the American jeep, firing burst after burst after burst.

Daniels watched him, fascinated. His body was being shredded by bullets. He was committing suicide.

Abernathy's voice blared in his ear.

"What's happening?"

"They tried to break out through the front."

"How many?"

"I don't know. Three. Four."

"Your men in position?"

"Should be."

The firing died down gradually.

Abernathy peered through the smoke and dust.

"What now?"

"I don't know. Do we close in?"

"No. Wait. We've got the place surrounded. There's no way out. We can wait."

"Captain, Captain." DiSalvo was out of breath, clutching his sides. "They took Peterson's jeep."

"Jesus."

Abernathy started to run after DiSalvo. Daniels followed. Peterson's body was lying in an alley behind the inn, where he'd parked. His throat had been cut. Nearby lay another man. He had been killed in the same silent way.

"Christ," Abernathy said. "It was a diversion."

They walked back to the square. GIs were pounding into the inn. The innkeeper was standing outside, blinking, trying to console two hysterical women. Behind thick, gray cloud, the sun was up.

Abernathy walked over to Legge's body. It was hardly recognizable as a body.

"God Almighty," Abernathy said. "Where's Stachek?"

The Czech was standing by the jeep. He shambled over to Abernathy.

"This one of them?"

Stachek stared at the corpse. There was hardly anything left of the face to identify it. He recognized some scraps of sandy, grayish hair.

"I think it's the one they called Legge," he said. "An Englishman."

"A goddamn Limey," Daniels said. "Would you believe it?"

Stachek was glowering. "I told you," he said. "These people are the best. Outnumbered two to one, three to one—and they got away."

Abernathy spat. "They won't get away a second time. You have my personal guarantee on that." He started to walk away. "Someone scrape that mess off the ground."

27

Bormann was listening with half an ear to Hitler's monologue. A dozen high-ranking officers were sitting in an almost religious silence as Hitler, raucous-voiced, continued, interrupted occasionally by a cough or a nose discreetly blown.

"For a long time now, I have marveled at the extreme differences among the Allies. On one hand, there are the capitalist countries; on the other, the Marxist countries. Then there's a dying British Empire and a former colony— the United States—ready to snatch the torch from her.

"Each partner in that alliance had the hope of achieving its own goal: the United States sought to inherit the British Empire; the Russians wanted the Balkans; the British were trying to hold sway over the Mediterranean. This is where we needed more time. I thought—we all thought—we would have enough time to hit them harder and harder. If we'd managed to do that, the Allies would have collapsed all by themselves. But time ran against us."

Bormann scratched his ear and avoided Hitler's baleful stare.

"None of you ever understood the truth. If the United States had thrown in the sponge, nothing would have happened. New York would have stayed New York; San Francisco would have stayed San Francisco. The German people thought they could do things the same way and said: 'We're fed up! We can't fight anymore.' That was when the Third Reich ceased to exist."

Hitler wandered over to the huge situation map of Europe and pondered silently. It was the moment Bormann had been waiting for. As discreetly as possible, he slipped through the audience and opened the door to the corridor. As it closed behind him, Hitler's voice could be heard:

"I always feared an Allied landing in Norway. . . ."

"I want two men to come with me," said Bormann.

Colonel Högl, who was watching the corridor, issued a curt command and two Leibstandarte SS men swung into step behind the Minister.

"If the Führer asks for me," Bormann went on, "tell him I'll be back in two hours." He went into the foyer and climbed stairs reserved for staff only. This led him to the emergency exit of the Führerbunker. Reaching the garden, he noticed the Signal Corps technicians hauling down their antennae-carrying balloon.

"Transmissions have become impossible," one of them explained. "The Russians use our balloon as a mark for adjusting artillery fire. It's become a menace for this whole area."

Bormann gave no reply. Keeping low, he hugged the walls of the old Chancellery and crossed its abandoned court. He came out on Voss-strasse.

A Kübelwagen stood waiting at the curb. Bormann climbed into the front seat. While one SS man took the wheel, the other stood on the running board.

"Gestapo Headquarters," Bormann ordered.

The Kübelwagen backfired, sputtered, then lurched forward. On Wilhelmstrasse, the SS man on the running board shouted to the driver and the vehicle went careering under a massive archway as a pair of low-flying Yak fighters unleashed random bursts of machine-gun fire before roaring away again.

Bormann realized that there were fewer heavy air raids on the center of Berlin now. It meant that the Red Army was contenting itself with harassing artillery fire and busily grouping its forces for the final assault.

They reached Prinz-Albrechtstrasse without further incident. A favorite target of the Russian batteries, the Gestapo HQ was little more than a ruin. But Bormann knew that, despite this, certain offices were still functioning in the extensive cellars.

"Wait for me as long as necessary," he said curtly. "Park the vehicle under an archway and don't leave here for any reason."

"Good day, Herr Reichsminister."

It was a small bespectacled man in civilian clothes, standing under an archway.

Bormann acknowledged him coldly and said quietly: "Take me to Eichmann immediately."

The little man nodded and preceded Bormann through the rubble. They made their way down to the cellars, marched briskly along the garishly lit corridors, and halted in front of a door marked with a brass plaque: IV-B-4.

Without bothering to knock, Bormann entered, closing the door behind him. The man seated at the desk, Herr Doktor Adolf Eichmann, looked up and gave his visitor a brief nod.

"I was expecting you later," he said, scribbling a note on a sheet of paper, which he slid into a drawer.

"Things are happening fast," Bormann replied. "What's going on here? It looks like you're operating with a skeleton crew."

"Monitoring and Transmissions was forced to move out. I've given them desk space at my building on Kurfürstendamm. With the generators and ventilating system over there, they'll be more comfortable than in the Führerbunker. And better protected from air raids."

"So you've been promoted, eh? Where is Kaltenbrunner?"

"He's awaiting the delivery of a baby."

"What?"

"His mistress is having a baby. He has been detained in Altraussee by this . . . affair of state."

"And Müller?"

"Very busy. I'm going to let you in on a little secret. My superior doesn't want it to get out, but our friend Heinrich Müller is playing his Bolshevik card. He's trying to save his own skin by postponing the execution of the last survivors of the Red Orchestra. Those Communist spies will be allowed to live until their friends get here."

"Nowadays," Bormann said, "we're all playing our last card."

"And yours—is me."

"Exactly. How is our plan progressing?"

The lights in the room dimmed for a moment, then came back on.

"Everything is ready."

He opened a drawer and withdrew a large envelope, which he handed to Bormann.

"Here are your papers—Herr Bauer."

"Bauer?"

"Richard Bauer. In a few days, I become Otto Klement. It's as simple as that. The envelope also contains information on the underground networks you can use to get out of Germany. The fastest, but also the most dangerous route is through Schleswig-Holstein. If you want my advice, go via Italy. The way I see it, you are required to stay in the bunker until the very last minute."

Bormann nodded.

"Let's say as soon as there is . . . no further reason for remaining," Eichmann continued, "you slip out of the bunker. Head for Kurfürstendamm. There you will receive help in leaving the city."

"And where will you be?"

Eichmann hesitated, then: "Everything is set for my departure. My underground network is ready."

"In that case nothing remains but to wish you good luck. Oh—one other matter," he added casually, "I placed a girl in Müller's care."

"Her name?" Eichmann reached for a typewritten list.

"Hellmann. Beate Hellmann. Aged seventeen."

"Being held for questioning?"

"No. For other reasons—which are no longer relevant. She can be released."

"Very well, I'll issue the instruction." Eichmann grimaced. "The way things are going, a seventeen-year-old girl will be safer in a cell."

28

The jeep jolted to a halt in front of the town hall. The two officers, one German, the other American, went quickly up the dozen or so steps leading to the main door of the building. Swastika flags had been replaced by the Stars and Stripes, but the Nazi emblems sculpted in the stone façade had yet to be smashed with sledgehammers.

Two MPs at the entrance threw the American officer smart salutes. With the German following close behind, he went down a long corridor. Muffled voices came from behind closed doors on which German lettering had been masked with cardboard signs. These were stenciled with the letters and code numbers of the various officers of the Seventh Army's G-2 section. The American stopped before a door, knocked twice, and entered. The German followed him in without a word. The General's adjutant cupped his hand over the telephone receiver he was holding and said, "The General will be a few minutes, Major. Take a seat."

General Stack was in the office of the Bürgermeister, which had been requisitioned for him. He had turned it into a combination sitting room, bedroom, and office. The General was leafing through a dossier on the British Corps. Its author, a young second lieutenant fresh out of Harvard, sat opposite.

"I'm impressed, Stanton," the General said, closing the file. "Good piece of work. Summarize, would you?"

"Well, sir, the Waffen SS was basically German at its inception," Stanton said, "but, with the outbreak of the war, this combat organization turned into a kind of foreign legion. According to our sources, there isn't a single Waffen SS division made up entirely of Germans. Our researchers have investigated thirty-eight divisions. Of these, eighteen were made up exclusively of foreigners; the rest were mixed. You have the list there. The divisions made up mainly of Germans were: the Leibstandarte, Adolf Hitler, Das Reich, Totenkopf verbände, Fourth Polizei, the Wiking, Nord, Prinz Eugen, Florian Geyer, Hohenstaufen, Frundsberg, Nordland, Hitlerjugend, Reichsführer SS, Götz von Berlichingen, Horst Wessel, Maria Theresa, and the Nibelungen. All the rest were composed largely of ethnic troops. The Handschar and Kama were Croat. The Fifteenth and Eighteenth were Letts. The Twentieth was Estonian, the Twenty-first Albanian. The Twenty-fifth and Thirty-third were Hungarian."

"Let's skip Eastern Europe and the Balkans," Stack cut in. "I'd rather have detailed information on the Western European units."

147

"Certainly, sir. The twenty-eighth is Walloon and the Thirty-third, which used to be Hungarian, was re-formed with French volunteers. That became the Charlemagne Division. Now, you've also got two Cossack cavalry units, a Serbian unit, two Rumanian ones, and the Twenty-ninth is Italian. We've also got small detachments of regimental strength, or less, like the Finnish volunteers, the Norwegian ski battalion and, finally, what concerns us, the British Free Corps.

"There's a big difference between the men of the British Corps and the other foreign volunteers in the Waffen SS. I'd be safe in saying that Waffen-SS troop strength has only undergone a serious buildup in recent months. Many combat and collaborator units fighting in the Wehrmacht were transferred to the SS a few months ago. Dutchmen, Belgians, Danes, Norwegians, and French. A few Swiss, Luxembourgers, and Swedes, as well. Now, the case of the English is quite different.

"For the Germans, the British Corps was mainly a propaganda move and actual recruitment didn't begin until 1943. Last year, the Englishmen of the BC asked to be commanded by Brigadier General Parrington, a first-rate officer captured in Greece in 1941. But we could find out nothing of Himmler's reaction to this."

"They sure didn't have much luck with their recruiting program," General Stack said. "Fifty men—that's nothing."

"Right, sir. That explains why the BC has never been attached to a regular unit. The report goes on to say— according to information received from escaped POWs— that the SS were in the habit of planting people in the stalags. These informers kept the Germans posted about the general attitude of POWs to the idea of a British legion. Any POW sympathizer would be given an immediate transfer out of the stalag and processed by their specialists. But the results were paltry."

"Okay," Stack said. "I think I'm beginning to get the picture. You've done a great job, Lieutenant. If Major Fenner's arrived, have him come in."

A moment later the door opened and Major Fenner saluted. Behind him stood the gaunt-looking German colonel, who wore horn-rimmed glasses.

"Come in, Fenner. Take a seat." He glanced at the German inquiringly.

"Colonel von Brauchitsch, General," Fenner said. "On the Göring matter."

"Von Brauchitsch," the German repeated stiffly, advancing a step. "Obviously you were informed of my arrival since the Major was waiting at the appointed place."

"That's right," Stack said. "Your original intermediary made the arrangements."

"I have come to speak to you directly on behalf of Marschall Göring. I am his aide-de-camp."

"The Marshal certainly takes precautions."

"Our negotiations must be highly confidential. Not to be divulged until the war is over. The Marschall is insistent on this point. He is in great danger."

"Even greater than you think," said Fenner. "Sit down, please."

Von Brauchitsch took a seat opposite Stack.

"Marshal Göring has been found guilty of treason," Fenner said. "He's been arrested on orders from Hitler."

"And transferred from Obersalzberg to Mauterndorf by the SS. I know this," von Brauchitsch said impatiently.

"Subsequently he was sentenced to death."

"But the SS either wouldn't or couldn't carry out the orders. And even if they intended to execute him, they didn't have time. A company of Luftwaffe parachutists arrived and escorted the Marschall from Mauterndorf to Radstadt, near Zell-am-See."

"Exactly. But what the Marshal didn't know—and what we ourselves didn't know until last night—is the fact that Hitler had taken precautions. A team of killers left from Berlin, via Czechoslovakia, to carry out the sentence. The group is—or, at least, was—made up of two Germans and five members of the Waffen SS British Free Corps."

Von Brauchitsch stared at Fenner, at once disturbed and suspicious.

"It's true," Stack said. "And it's given us a problem. I have to protect your Marshal; we want him alive—for intelligence purposes. I also have to protect myself. I can't have any goddamned press leaks. British fighting alongside the SS in the last hours of the war, moving freely through our area, dressed up in GI uniforms! Jesus! Plus they happen to have killed ten of my men in the last twenty-four hours."

Fenner nodded.

"For the time being," he said, "only a few people know the secret. The General and myself, as well as ten or twelve GIs in a forward position a mile or two from Mauterndorf. If we can maintain secrecy for another few hours, we can bury the whole thing when we bury those British Corps sons of bitches."

"How do you plan to do that?" von Brauchitsch inquired.

"That's where you and the Marshal come in. We protect him by stopping the British. In exchange, Göring gets our assurance that the terms of his surrender will be respected."

"To keep his public image intact, Marschall Göring doesn't want news of his surrender divulged until after the armistice, once the hostilities have officially ended."

"Agreed," said Stack promptly. "Now, we've got to get busy. What are the latest reports like, Fenner?"

"Abernathy and Lieutenant Daniels' I and R section are waiting in that village. They've lost two men and a jeep."

Stack spread a large situation map over his desk.

"We're here and the village is there. Considering the place where Marshal Göring is right now, is there any way of getting to that spot very rapidly, Colonel? That is, of course, without running into regular Wehrmacht units still fighting in the sector?"

Von Brauchitsch hesitated, then answered: "I can guide your men. But it's possible that the killers are already near their objective."

"They're almost certainly there," Fenner said. "But they won't try the main roads in daylight. We know that none of our own reconnaissance patrols are moving within these co-ordinates. The General has requested close tactical support from the Air Corps. In fact, they have orders to strafe any suspect vehicle on the roads. That should force our friends to move only by night."

"That is, if they still intend to carry out their mission," the German said. "They may have deserted already. It would be in character."

"Unfortunately, we can't make that assumption," Stack said. "I can't risk it. So you will accompany Major Fenner to the village where Abernathy and his men are waiting. Then you take them to the Marshal's hideout.

They'll be responsible for taking out the killers if they show."

"There is just one thing," said von Brauchitsch. "You must give me your word as an officer that once this matter has been settled, the Marschall will be given freedom of movement until the armistice."

"You have my word," Stack said shortly. "Okay, Fenner, carry on."

Fenner and von Brauchitsch walked out into the courtyard that served as a motor pool for the GHQ. A Dodge four-by-four was waiting, one man at the wheel, two more in the backseat.

"Sergeant Floyd, sir," announced the driver. "That's Larkin and McInerny."

"You're OSS, right?"

"Right, Major. We've got our gear all set—take a look."

He jerked his thumb at two silencer-equipped Thompson submachine guns and two carbines lying on the seat. From his shoulder holster jutted the butt of a Colt .45.

"You boys travel light," Fenner remarked. Then he unfolded a situation map and pointed to a winding pencil line. "This marks the first leg of our trip. We've got to get there as fast as possible. We'll be covered all the way by spotter planes from the Air Corps. Let's move out."

29

"We can't possibly proceed in this," Hellmann said.

The fog was swirling round the jeep so densely that O'Mara had been forced to pull off the road, down a track that led to a ruined barn.

"On the contrary," Wrack said. "It is providential. The Americans will never find us in it."

"We'll find *them*," O'Mara said. "We'll run right into the back of a Sherman tank or slap into a roadblock. You can't see your hand in front of your face."

"We're on low ground," Wrack said. "We have only to climb a few meters and the fog will clear."

"Makin' us sitting ducks."

O'Mara spat and fumbled for a cigarette. He was leaning against the remains of a wall, his Sten propped beside him. Wrack had told Hellmann what had happened at the inn and had warned him: "Allow O'Mara to abort this mission and that's it for your sister."

O'Mara, who had, of course, listened to their entire conversation, with a grin on his face, had said: "Don't worry, Lieutenant. I'll do your dirty work for you, if it's that keen you are."

Hellmann glanced at Wrack. Wrack was holding his Schmeisser in a way that made it clear he was prepared to use it instantly. For the hundredth time Hellmann wondered if there was any way of persuading the SS Lieutenant to abandon the mission, if there were any arguments that could pierce his fanaticism.

"I agree with O'Mara," Hellmann said. "We escaped from the village by a miracle. We won't get two miracles."

"We escaped from the village with this," Wrack said, touching his dagger. "If I have this, I don't need miracles. You had your orders direct from the Führer himself, Captain, but apparently that means nothing to you. I'm not surprised. The Army was always rotten with traitors. But I remind you that you have no choice in the matter. Nor you." He turned to O'Mara. O'Mara shrugged awkwardly.

"When we have completed our task," Wrack went on, "I will lead you to the hunting lodge. From there I can contact Berlin and your sister will be released, Captain. You, O'Mara, will get what you want. After that, what you do is of no concern to me."

Hellmann suddenly understood Wrack. The man was an automaton, a clockwork creature that the SS had manufactured and wound up. Until the mechanism ran down—in other words, until Wrack was dead—the creature would go on and on. It was pointless trying to change it, divert it: its responses were pre-set.

He turned away and walked over to the jeep. Erika was huddled in the front seat, half asleep.

"Look," Hellmann said quietly. "We're going to go on. We have no choice. But you should stay here."

She shook her head.

"Erika—I can't protect you. If you stay with me you'll be committing suicide. Wrack won't object. He knows there's nothing you can do. Wait here until the fog lifts, then find a farm, or a village. You'll be all right." He forced

154

a smile. "You can take care of yourself."

"And then what?"

Hellmann hesitated; he didn't understand.

"How will you find me again? How will I find you?"

Again he hesitated.

"Perhaps you wouldn't want to find me again?" she said.

"Of course I would," he said—and instantly regretted it. For her own sake he should have pretended indifference. Then she might have agreed to stay behind. As it was . . .

"Then I must stay with you. I'm not afraid. Whatever I do I'll be running into danger. I feel safe with you."

Hellmann laughed wryly. After all, what the hell did it really matter? Nothing made sense anymore.

"It's all crazy anyway," she said, reading his thoughts.

Wrack came up. "The fog's lifting a little. We must get on. We've wasted enough time."

"What will you do, Wrack?" Hellmann asked. "When it's over. I mean when everything's over. The Third Reich. The SS. Everything."

Wrack didn't answer. Instead he barked at O'Mara: "Come on."

O'Mara trod out his cigarette and grinned at Hellmann. "For the likes of Wrack," he said, "and me too, you could say nothing's ever over."

30

The hunting lodge was a late-nineteenth-century folly, a one-room timber building with a thatched roof and a veranda supported with pseudo-rustic beams. The walls, and the shutters of the lugubrious Gothic windows, had once been brightly painted with "peasant" patterns. After years of neglect, the paintwork was peeling, and the thatch, rotten and sagging, had the appearance of a manure heap.

A squat, thickset man, with a cropped brush of black hair, was standing on the veranda. He was scanning the surrounding countryside through a pair of Zeiss field glasses. The hunting lodge stood alone, in a sparse clump of trees, at the top of a hill. It was the highest point for some miles, commanding sweeping views of the thickly forested valley and the undulating fields beyond.

The valley and the forest were still wreathed in thick fog, but on higher ground there remained only hazy wisps of the blanket that, an hour earlier, had blotted out everything.

The man with the field glasses scanned methodically from east to west, then from west to east, concentrating on the three tracks that meandered up the hill, through plantations of pine, and converged at the hunting lodge.

Inside the building, another man sat at a stout oak table. His appearance was identical to that of the man on the veranda. They were brothers, identical twins. They were also partners in the business of professional killing, and for several years they had been employed by the Sicherheitsdienst, the SS security service. An active, enjoyable, lucrative employment.

The man opened a small, square leather suitcase and began setting out its contents on the table. The contents were a complete forger's outfit: rubber stamps, specimen signatures, seals, and identity documents of several nations and types—civilian, military, diplomatic—with the details left blank. There was also a pile of photographs of various shapes and sizes. The photographs were of members of the British Corps: Ward, Chandra, Legge, and the others. There were at least a dozen different shots of each.

The man pulled a metal cashbox toward him. He unlocked it and riffled through the neat bundles of ten-pound notes. A lot of money. And genuine, not counterfeit.

He smiled, and glanced at the powerful transmitter-receiver in the corner. Bormann's message had got through all right. Sanction.

His brother came in from the veranda.

"Any coffee?"

"On the stove."

"What are you grinning about?"

The other closed the lid of the cashbox. "Any sign of them?"

"Nothing. But it's early yet."

"I wonder how many'll get through?"

"Not many. Two. Three at most. Shouldn't be too difficult to deal with them."

"No."

"Bit of luck for us."

"Yes."

"Where do you fancy? Have you thought? Spain?"

"Why not? See some sunshine. And we've got good friends in Madrid."

"Yes." He sipped at his coffee, then grinned. His brother responded. Often they could read each other's minds with complete accuracy. It was what made them such a formidable team.

"It's quite exciting."

"Yes. Quite exciting."

31

The huge Opel "Blitz" had straddled the road, its right front tire half flat. The driver scratched his head and scowled. They were overloaded—that was the problem.

"We haven't got far to go," he said, turning to Emil. "We should make it—just. I can't risk changing a wheel with all that weight in the rear. Anyway I don't even know if I have a lug wrench."

Göring's manservant sighed. "The Marschall will be furious if any of his things are damaged."

"Let him move his own junk. This is the fourth trip already and I've had it up to here." He touched the top of his head and spat. Emil was about to put him in his place when the sound of an approaching vehicle made him whip round.

The American jeep was braking hard, with a squeal of rubber. Emil's stomach churned—but then he remembered the deal his master had made—had boasted about in his usual way. Perhaps . . .

The GIs were eyeing him curiously. One of them turned and spoke to his companions in rapid English. Very tentatively Emil moved forward toward the jeep.

"Do you speak German?" he said, raising his arms.

One of the GIs nodded, and raised his machine pistol menacingly.

"Don't shoot," Emil said in German. "We're noncombatants. Civilians."

The American didn't look as if he were about to shoot and Emil stepped closer to the jeep. Lowering his voice, he said: "Look. I think I know where you're going. To . . . a certain important person, *nicht wahr*?"

The American did not answer immediately. A cautious individual, Emil thought. After a moment, the American said: "That's right. What do you know about it?"

"I'm the Marschall's personal manservant," Emil explained eagerly.

"I see."

"Yes," Emil said. "I know all about it. I am in the Marschall's confidence."

"I understand," the American said. "You have a responsible position. Perhaps you could help us. I think we have missed our way."

"No, no. This is the right road."

"What's happened to your truck?"

"A flat tire. Not completely flat." He smiled ingratiatingly. "We have a heavy load, you see. Part of the Marschall's collection."

"We could follow you," the American said.

One of the others, the driver, was pulling a pack of American cigarettes out of his pocket. The German-speaking one said: "Would you like some cigarettes?"

Emil accepted them delightedly.

"If we follow you and you have any more trouble, we could help out. Is it far?"

"No, no. A few miles. Thank you." He hesitated. Then he added: "There are not very many of you. I think the Marschall is expecting more."

"We came on ahead. The others are only half an hour behind."

"Oh. I see. Well then." He was about to move back to the truck when he thought it might be prudent to compliment the American on his flawless command of German. He did so—fulsomely.

"I studied German, in America. I was going to take my degree when this lousy war came along."

Emil smiled. "Ah well. It's nearly over now. For all of us."

The American smiled back. For such a hard-looking man he seemed very friendly.

When Emil was out of earshot, climbing into the cab of the truck, the driver of the jeep grinned and said, in a broad Irish brogue: "That was quick thinking, Lieutenant."

Wrack almost managed a smile.

"It's providence," he said. "Göring's obviously been

moved. This will save us valuable time."

Emil was waving an arm out of the window of the cab. Wrack waved back. The engine of the truck fired and the ungainly vehicle moved forward slowly.

"Keep as close as you can," Wrack told O'Mara.

The jeep moved off in the wake of the truck.

"He's going to lead us right up to Göring's door." Wrack was exultant.

"That swine," he said, after a moment. "How right the Führer was. He's finally sold himself to the Americans. But not soon enough. Not soon enough."

"We don't know that," Hellmann said. "The servant's been out of touch. The Americans may have already arrived. The place could be swarming with them."

"I don't care if there's a regiment," Wrack said. "It won't stop me."

O'Mara half turned.

"They'll think we're escorting the truck," he said. "By the time they realize their mistake it'll be too late."

He seemed to be as keen as Wrack.

Hellmann turned to Wrack. "Listen, we must make some kind of plan. We can't just drive in . . ."

"From now on, Hellmann," Wrack said, "you'll take your orders from me. I will know how to handle it."

32

"My wife would be honored if you and your officers would share our humble meal," Göring said.

The Marschall was resplendent in a black velvet suit.

"Thank you," Major Fenner said, "but we are responsible for protecting you and I don't have many men."

"I understand," said Göring. "I was a soldier myself. Do you know that in 1915 I managed to down one of the first Handley-Page bombers ever to come out of the English aircraft factories? I was commanding one of the best squadrons in the world. Men like von Richthofen and Reinhardt had led the outfit before me. Heroes. Real heroes."

"Excuse me, sir," Fenner interrupted, smoothly, "I have to speak to Captain Abernathy."

"Of course," said Göring, dismissing him with a regal gesture.

A shabby lot, Americans, he thought as he watched the Major move away. Not even clean, let alone smart. Amateurs.

He walked over to the crates stacked in a corner of the drawing room and stooped to read the labels: Matisse, Soutine, Degas, Utrillo, Renoir, Monet, Cézanne, Pissarro.

In the adjoining room, his collection of rare coins

was spread out on a table: gold Hebrew shekels, Greek tetradrachmas, Roman sesterces . . . He fingered them lovingly.

"There are still the rugs, the porcelains, my collection of Florentine statues," he said to his wife, who had entered and was watching him in silence. "The Luftwaffe really could have lent a hand with the moving when they brought us here."

"Their trucks were full. Just thank God that they got us away from the SS."

"But they soon abandoned us," he said with a sigh.

"You still have Brauchitsch and Koller. They're loyal."

"Where are they?"

"In the pantry. Is Emil back?"

"No, not yet. I hope nothing's gone wrong. He's bringing my rugs. By the way, what do you think of them?"

"Your rugs?"

"The Americans. How do they strike you?"

"They're gentlemen. Quite mannerly, quite correct. Frankly, I wasn't expecting them to be so well behaved."

"The French are the vulgar ones. If only you knew the English! They are perfect. Better than the Americans. Did I ever tell you about that British flier who became my friend after the war?"

"Yes, Hermann, a thousand times. Come on. Lunch is ready."

The house in which Göring, his family, and staff had taken refuge belonged to a wealthy landowner who had fled two months earlier. The main building was L-shaped, built round a courtyard full of flower beds.

Fenner and Abernathy had posted their men so that they covered the entire courtyard. Floyd, Larkin, and

McInerny were stationed in the barn, where the vehicles were camouflaged. Daniels, Stachek, and two privates were assigned to the toolshed. Eight other soldiers had been spread around the main building to protect Göring and his family. The dispositions would have been approved by any field general. It was set up for a classic ambush. There was only one problem. The fog.

Without Colonel von Brauchitsch, who knew the region perfectly, the Americans would never have reached Radstadt before noon. All the way Major Fenner, peering blindly through the windshield of his jeep, had cursed the fog. It prevented the observation planes from doing their job, and had slowed them to a crawl. But they'd arrived, intact and more or less on time, but the fog hadn't lifted—and it worried him. He moved restlessly between the various positions, encouraging his men, smoking a cigarette with Floyd, exchanging banter with Daniels. Abernathy didn't seem concerned.

"Relax, Major," he said. "Cigarette?"

Fenner accepted a cigarette.

"The way I figure it," Abernathy went on, "either they've given up or they're driving around in circles in the goddamn fog. They won't make it here until the fog's lifted. And with no fog, we've got 'em cold."

"I guess that's right, Major," Daniels said.

"Don't be too sure," Stachek growled. "A bit of fog isn't going to stop a man like Wrack."

"I'm sending out a patrol when the fog lifts," Fenner said. "I'm not taking any chances."

"They'll be here," Stachek said. "You take my word for it. Just remember. Wrack is mine."

The big Opel seemed to be slowing down. Wrack sensed

that they were almost at their destination.

"Right," Wrack said, and his voice betrayed tension. "You, Hellmann, stay by the jeep. Cover the two in the truck. I doubt it, but they may try something when the shooting starts. The girl stays in the jeep. You keep the engine running, of course. O'Mara and I will enter the house. We will find Göring and kill him as swiftly as possible. Your job, Hellmann, is to be ready to get us out fast."

Hellmann's instinct as a soldier was to challenge Wrack. To attempt such an operation without reconnaissance was idiotic. Göring could have fifty SS guarding him. Or fifty GIs for that matter. They knew nothing about the house. It could be some mansion with a hundred rooms and Göring could be locked up in a cellar or an attic. He could be in the bath, or sitting on the toilet. He understood Wrack's thinking. The element of surprise. Göring was expecting to see Americans. But there were too many unknown factors to weigh against that.

But he said nothing. There was no point. Wrack wouldn't listen. Anyway, he could be right. He turned to look at Erika, crouched in the back. He smiled at her, trying to reassure her, then turned to O'Mara as the Irishman hissed: "Lodge gates. This is it."

Wrack flipped his safety. Hellmann followed suit.

Ahead, the truck was picking up a little speed. Dimly, through the swirls of thick fog, they could make out a line of trees on either side of a narrow drive.

Just as I thought, Hellmann said to himself, a mansion. Let's hope to God it's not too huge.

"You think it's lifting at all?" Fenner was asking Abernathy.

Suddenly Stachek stiffened. "What's that?"

They listened, instantly tense. The grinding roar of the Opel's motor came through the fog.

"This is it," Daniels said hoarsely, hefting his gun.

"It's a truck," Stachek stated, with an edge of disappointment and frustration.

"God Almighty," Abernathy said, as the truck loomed through the fog and slowed down with harsh shrieks of its brakes, "it's Göring's goddamn moving van."

The truck halted, its tires spitting gravel.

"Tell the driver to park round the back," Fenner said. "He's screwing up our field of fire."

Abernathy took a step forward. But Daniels's hand clamped onto his upper arm in an agonizing grip. Daniels was staring . . . at another vehicle emerging from the fog, slowing, halting. . . .

"Jesus Christ, that's Peterson's jeep," he said. "It's them."

O'Mara wrenched on the hand brake and was out of the jeep, swinging his Sten with him, before it was fully stationary. Wrack had jumped out even sooner and was striding toward the house. O'Mara was a pace behind him when machine-gun fire erupted from one side of the courtyard.

O'Mara hit the ground and rolled for the cover of the truck. He was briefly aware of Emil and the truck driver standing together a few yards from him, paralyzed, and then he was squeezing off burst after burst in the direction of the enemy fire.

At the first shots Wrack had started to run toward the house. There were machine pistols blazing from three sides of the courtyard now. He reached the wall of the house unscathed, and dropped. Ahead of him loomed a projecting wing. He could make out a line of French windows. He began to creep toward them.

Hellmann was cut down as he stepped out of the jeep, in the first hail of fire. Agony exploded in his thigh, his shoulder, and, unendurably, his hand. He was smashed against the side of the jeep and hit the ground, unable to control animal shrieks of pain from the wound in his hand. Then some sort of cloth was crammed into his mouth and he felt himself being dragged toward the cover of the rear end of the jeep. Erika.

Then he blacked out.

Göring had been raising a chicken leg to his mouth when the shooting started. For a moment he had stared dumbly at his wife, at Koller, at Brauchitsch.

Then, without knowing what he was doing, he had risen in his chair, still holding the chicken leg, gaping at the French windows opposite.

Somebody screamed: "Down! Get down!"

Behind him, the door crashed open and two of the Americans burst in.

As they did so, the French windows seemed to explode.

Göring dropped to the floor.

Crouching under the table, he saw one of the Americans reeling backward, his face lacerated by flying glass, jets of blood pumping hideously from his neck.

Wrack backed away from the French windows. Through the shattered glass and woodwork and the ripped curtains he had a glimpse of an ornately furnished dining room, then a burst of fire from within the room forced him to dive and crawl away.

He started to run the way he had come, back to the jeep.

O'Mara had wormed his way under the truck to the

front. Emil and the driver were lying on the ground, their arms over their heads. The courtyard was a crazy inferno of flying lead.

O'Mara counted to three, then gripped the running board from the underneath, hauled himself out from under the truck, wrenched the door open, and slid into the driver's seat. Bullets drilled into the metalwork as he fired the engine. The windshield shattered. He jammed into gear and stamped the throttle, hauling on the wheel.

As the truck jolted forward, Wrack dived. A steel-tipped bullet tore through his forearm, but he clung to the door of the truck, fighting to get it open. The truck heeled over as it turned to head for the drive, and the door swung open with Wrack still holding on to it. He was hit again, but superficially, in the thigh, and as the truck gathered speed, he swung himself inside.

As the truck vanished into the fog, Stachek darted out of cover.

He heard Abernathy yell: "Come back here, you crazy son of a bitch!" but he ignored him. At a crouch, he ran for the jeep.

Someone, Fenner probably, was screaming at the men to cease firing.

Stachek jumped into the jeep. The engine was still running. He tried gears wildly, found first, and let in the clutch. The jeep shot forward, executed a ninety-degree skid-turn and rocketed away, into the fog.

"Pull in over there, into the trees," Wrack said. He had bandaged his arm with a piece of his shirt. It was a clean wound. And it was his left arm. The other wound, in his thigh, was nothing—a graze.

O'Mara jammed on the brakes and swung the heavy

truck off the road. The wheels bounced over roots and he had to fight for control. It gave Wrack the opportunity he had been waiting for to seize O'Mara's Sten, lying between them on the seat.

O'Mara read Wrack's movement a second too late. He stamped on the brakes, but Wrack had already braced himself.

"All right," Wrack said. "Get out."

O'Mara climbed stiffly out of the truck. Wrack followed.

Rays of strong sunlight were penetrating the fog in places, but visibility was still minimal.

O'Mara was shaking his head. "Well, wouldn't you know it. After all that and you're going to kill me."

"No," Wrack said. "I still need you. We're going back."

O'Mara gaped at him, for once totally dumbfounded.

"I am certain that Göring is still alive," Wrack said. "I failed to get into the house."

O'Mara laughed shortly and scratched his head.

"You know," he said, "Ward was right about you. First time he saw you he said you were mad, dangerously mad."

Wrack said nothing.

"Do you really think I'm going back there? I'd rather die here—get it over with quickly."

"You don't want to die, O'Mara. You want to survive. I still hold the key to your survival."

"Listen, boyo," O'Mara said. "I can do my sums, you know. If we go back, what'll happen? One, we both die. Two, I die and you survive. Three, you die and I survive. But if you're dead, I don't get my new passport or my money, so I might as well be dead. Look at it any way you want—it's bad business."

"We might both survive," Wrack said.

"Not a chance."

There was another silence.

"Listen, Wrack, be reasonable, would you now," O'Mara said. "You did your best. Holy Mother, nobody coulda done more. But it's impossible, don't you see. Now, somewhere near here there's a nice new set of papers and a pile of money waiting for us both. You know where. Why don't we just go there, Wrack? If it was the Führer himself standing here, he'd say the same."

O'Mara had reckoned that gentle persuasion stood the least chance of all of shifting Wrack, but, almost unbelievably, a look of doubt had crept into the Lieutenant's eyes. O'Mara thought fast.

"Listen. We've got one weapon between us and there's half an army defendin' that house. But at the hunting lodge now, there's a radio. You can contact Berlin. Maybe they can send some men. We know where Göring is. They won't move him for a few hours if at all. Maybe they could bomb the place." Sweet Christ, make him see reason.

Wrack's tongue flicked over his lips.

"Possibly you are right." He was silent for a long time, during which O'Mara called on Sweet Christ again and again.

At last Wrack said: "Very well. But I may still require you."

"If there's half a chance of succeeding, I'll go along with you," O'Mara said.

"Very well. We must proceed on foot. It is not far."

From a pocket he produced a small compass. He looked at the road, at the compass, then at a straight path that led away into the pines.

"You go first," he said. "That way."

"*Halt.*"

Stachek's voice.

Wrack disobeyed. He swung the Sten round in the direction of the voice, squeezing the trigger.

Then something like a steamroller slammed him, blind and winded, to the ground.

O'Mara had drop-kicked him from behind. He rolled for the Sten.

"No."

Stachek emerged from cover, leveling a Garand M-1. "I've got no quarrel with you, O'Mara. Stand back."

O'Mara picked himself up and backed away.

Wrack was recovering. He fought for breath with a high-pitched wheezing that gradually subsided.

"Get up," Stachek ordered.

Shakily, Wrack got to his feet.

O'Mara was making a rapid calculation. He knew that the hunting lodge was not far away, probably less than two miles. He knew the general direction in which it lay. Did he have enough information to find it without Wrack's guidance? He decided that he did, and that therefore there was no point in trying to prevent Stachek from killing Wrack.

"Do you want me to help you finish this bastard?" O'Mara asked.

His eyes on Wrack, Stachek said: "I'm not interested in what you do. You're as good as dead anyway."

"That's right, O'Mara," Wrack croaked. "When he's killed me, he'll kill you."

"The Americans will deal with O'Mara. Unless he can escape."

Cautiously O'Mara began to step away. Wrack knew

171

that his only chance was if the Irishman's movements distracted Stachek for a second.

"I'm backing away, Stachek," O'Mara was saying. "I'm getting out."

Wrack made his move.

But Stachek's attention had not been diverted, even for a fraction of a second.

The eight-round clip in his Garand was as a single, prolonged explosion. Wrack's body was picked up like a leaf in the wind, dismembered, and flung, an unrecognizable pulp, against the trunk of a tree.

Stachek walked forward, reloading his Garand. He stared down at what was left of Wrack.

"Mother of God." O'Mara's voice sounded awed. He moved toward Wrack's body as if mesmerized by the hideous sight.

"It was a quick death," Stachek said. "Too good for him."

"Would you look at him, now," O'Mara said, squatting by Wrack. "I've never seen anything like *that*. No."

O'Mara straightened his knees, rising beside Stachek. In his right hand was Wrack's dagger, which the Irishman's sharp eye had seen drop into a tussock of grass as Wrack's body had hit the tree.

The blade flashed once across Stachek's throat and O'Mara caught the Garand neatly as it fell from the Czech's hands.

Stachek's body fell across Wrack's. The two corpses lay together, in an embrace, under the pine tree.

And O'Mara walked away, down the path, the Garand slung over one shoulder, the Sten over the other, whistling softly.

33

"No," Fenner said. "And that's a direct order, Abernathy."

"But, Christ, Major . . ."

"Abernathy, I'm not going to risk losing another man. Until this fog lifts nobody moves from here. I'm not having any patrols stumbling about in this goddamn pea soup being shot at and having their throats slit. No, sir. When it's clear—"

"When it's clear," Abernathy cut in bitterly, "it'll be too damned late."

"No it won't. Because I'll have half a division and half the Air Corps out gunning for those bastards and there's no way they're going to get away. I have the General's full backing." He laid a hand on Abernathy's arm and said, more gently: "Look, Abernathy. I know how you feel. But the war's going to be over in a few days, maybe less. I can't risk the lives of my men if the risk can be minimized in any way. Some of my guys have come through three years of it. I don't want them to die from a sniper's bullet in a fog because I couldn't wait an hour."

"Okay, Major," Abernathy said after a moment. "I guess you're right at that. Maybe the Czech got a couple of them."

"Maybe. How's our guest?"

Abernathy shrugged. "Still eating lunch."

"I'd better talk to him."

"The Führer," Göring was saying as Fenner entered the library, to which the Marschall and the others had retreated to finish their lunch, "has a sense of humor. At least, he had. I'll never forget the time when he gave the Grand Mufti in Jerusalem a bullet-proof vest!"

He laughed heartily and Koller and Brauchitsch stitched smiles onto their faces.

Göring waved Fenner to a chair, congratulating him on the splendid fight his men had put up. Fenner punctured his high spirits by remarking sourly: "We didn't kill any of them, so far as we know. They may be back."

But Göring soon recovered, pressing a liqueur on Fenner, and launching into more reminiscences.

"I knew we'd lost the war a few days after the Normandy landings. Simultaneously, the Russians launched their grand offensive and the British and Americans broke through at Avranches. In my opinion, that was the turning point—the air war. I told the Führer over and over again. Round-the-clock bombing—that's the only way to break a country's will. Crush them with bombs, destroy the factories, the marshaling yards, the roads." He stopped to top up his glass. "Aviation is the force of tomorrow. Bombers, give me bombers—that's what I always said . . . ."

He started to talk about his postwar plans. "I think I'll make a valuable conference partner for the Allies. Churchill has always said: 'Why don't they send me that fellow Göring instead of that gloomy von Ribbentrop?' May I ask you a question, Major?"

"Sure."

174

"What is the latest news from Berlin?"

"It's only a matter of hours."

"I see. And the Führ—and Hitler?"

"I haven't heard anything."

Göring sighed, then picked up his glass, seeking, and appearing to find, consolation in brandy.

34

APRIL 30, 1945, 2:00 P.M.

Three women were lunching with the Führer: his two secretaries, Gertrude Junge and Gerda Christian, and his cook, Constanze Manzialy. They ate spaghetti and a tossed salad, mostly in silence. But toward the end of the meal, Hitler became more conversational.

"I've always been pleased with your work. All of you. I have made arrangements for you. You've been excellent workers and I wish to help you even though my life is ending." Frau Junge's eyes filled with tears. Hitler turned away from the sight, got to his feet, and shuffled out.

He remained in his own quarters for more than half an hour. Then, with his wife on his arm, he entered the conference room, where sixteen members of his staff were gathered. The final roster of the faithful was: Goebbels;

Bormann; Generals Krebs and Burgdorf; Walter Hewel; Admiral Voss; Professor Haase; General Rattenhuber; Colonel Högl; Linge, Hitler's faithful valet; Major Günsche; the two secretaries who had lunched with him; Fräulein Krüger, Bormann's secretary; Constanze Manzialy; Werner Naumann. The most conspicuously absent face was that of Magda Goebbels.

Hitler made a short announcement, in a voice so subdued it was barely audible.

"I have decided to end it today. Now. I have seen too many failures, too many betrayals, to hope for any more of National Socialism or the German people."

Methodically he and Eva shook hands with everyone, and when the ceremony was over there was one of those long, crawling silences that had been such a feature of bunker life from the first.

Hitler at last glanced at Linge. The valet, trained to interpret his master's smallest gestures, saved the situation. He marched to the double doors leading to Hitler's quarters and opened them smartly.

With an awkward gesture of his right hand Hitler indicated that his wife should precede him. It was the gesture of an Austrian nobody with aspirations to being a gentleman. Eva Hitler disappeared through the door and Hitler followed. But before vanishing for the last time, he paused and clasped Linge's hand.

"Linge, my old friend," he said, "you must try to break out with the others."

Linge was startled. "But . . . but why, my Führer?"

"Because you must serve the one who comes after me."

Then the door closed.

They waited. The Führer's instructions had been clear. Wait for ten minutes.

They waited.

Linge was the first to crack. Choking, and muttering incoherently, he ran across the conference room, up the main stairs, out into the garden.

His astonishing departure was swiftly succeeded by a no less astonishing arrival.

Magda Goebbels appeared, her hair wild, her eyes red-rimmed from crying.

She ran toward the door to Hitler's quarters, demanding wildly to see the Führer.

Günsche barred her way, drawing his pistol.

"I'm sorry. The Führer cannot be disturbed."

"But I must see him. I must. I beg of you."

Günsche looked at the others—Bormann, Krebs, Goebbels himself—for guidance, but their expressions said nothing.

His face ashen, Günsche stepped to the door and knocked once. He opened the door. There was the sound of running water.

"My Führer," Günsche began. But Magda Goebbels pushed past him.

Günsche could not make out what was said distinctly, only that Hitler refused to speak to Frau Goebbels and ordered her out of his room. A moment later she emerged, weeping hysterically, stumbled past her husband, without looking at him, and disappeared.

As she left, Artur Axmann arrived, with his aide Günther Weltzin. Axmann strode toward the door of Hitler's suite, but this time Günsche was adamant.

"No. It's too late. Too late for anything."

They waited.

The sound of a revolver shot penetrated the fireproof and gasproof double doors.

At the sound of the shot, Linge reentered the conference room. He appeared to have regained control over himself, but his face looked ghastly, almost blue.

"It is time," he said in a half-whisper. "It is surely time."

He looked at the others. Nobody stirred.

Linge approached the door as a man approaches his own grave. He opened it and went in. The strong fumes of cordite and cyanide made his eyes water instantly. He backed out.

Bormann entered the room, followed by Linge, Günsche, Goebbels, and Axmann.

Hitler and his wife lay together on a small sofa, upholstered in blue and white velvet. Eva Hitler was unmarked. She lay with her feet tucked under her. Her high-heeled shoes and a pink silk scarf, carefully folded, were under the sofa.

Hitler's face was a gaping wound from which blood still dripped. He had slumped forward, and a heavy Walther 7.65 pistol lay on the floor nearby.

Bormann, with his habit of accuracy, thought: He shot himself and simultaneously bit into the cyanide capsule. Otherwise he would still be holding the pistol. The poison killed him.

A small Dresden vase had somehow fallen onto the carpet. Flowers, tulips and white narcissi, were strewn on the floor.

Linge, the eternal servant, suddenly stooped, picked up the vase, gathered the flowers, replaced them in the vase, and set it down on a side table, next to the small pistol that had belonged to Eva Hitler.

Linge's action broke the tension.

"Günsche, get some men in here," Bormann ordered.

There was general movement. Linge, who had left the room, now returned, carrying two coarse blankets.

Almost tenderly, he shrouded the bodies of Adolf and Eva Hitler.

35

"I can't," Hellmann said through teeth clenched against the agony in his thigh. "I can't make it any further. Go on. Leave me."

"Just a little further. We must get off the road. Just a little way. I'll help you."

They had improvised a crutch out of an old branch. Erika threw it aside and hooked Hellmann's left arm over her shoulder. Together they staggered off the road, into the forest.

Hellmann had blacked out only for a few seconds. When consciousness surged back, and with it unendurable pain, he had found that Erika was dragging him away from the jeep, dragging his big, heavy body with a strength born of desperation and made possible only because she had spent her life in manual work on a farm. Her determination had triggered his will to survive. Somehow he had managed to start crawling. Then, with

Erika supporting most of his weight, he had stumbled toward the dim outline of a grove of trees.

With the sound of the gun battle in the courtyard muffled by the fog, they had lurched across a paddock, splashed through a shallow stream, and had then been confronted by the high brick wall of a park. Without Erika, Hellmann could never have scaled that wall. At one point his whole weight was on her as he stood on her shoulders, groping for the top of the wall with his undamaged hand.

The gunfire had ceased suddenly as they limped into the forest. But they had found the going too rough and had taken to the road, ready to make a run for the trees at the approach of a U.S. patrol. But no patrols had appeared.

"What's that?" Erika said. "There, ahead."

Hellmann dropped to his knees—it was relief—and peered. There was no doubt. The jeep.

"You must scout," he whispered. "I'm sorry. I just can't move quietly."

"All right. I won't be long."

She wormed forward, through scrub, disappearing from his view. She made no sound. Hellmann thanked God she was country-bred. Three or four minutes passed and she reappeared, from another direction, walking upright. She squatted beside him.

"I'm certain there's nobody there. It's our jeep, all right. It's riddled with bullet holes."

She helped him forward. The jeep was standing in a small clearing from which a rough track led off in the direction of the road.

In the jeep lockers they found water, brandy, a first-aid kit, cigarettes, tins of corned beef.

Erika cleaned and dressed his wounds. The brandy

helped to numb the various throbbing pains in his thigh, shoulder, and hand.

"I think you've been lucky," Erika said. "They're clean wounds."

"*Lucky?*"

They both laughed. Hellmann inhaled deeply on a cigarette. He felt one hundred percent better.

"I suppose we are lucky," he said. "We're still alive. I wonder how lucky the others were."

"Well, one of them's still walking. There are tracks leading off into the forest. One set only."

"Erika, you're a marvel."

"I'm a country girl. My father used to take me hunting."

"Like to bet on who it is? Wrack is my guess."

"No," she said. "If only one got out, it would have been O'Mara. What do we do? Take the jeep?"

"Too risky. We'll follow the tracks. The hunting lodge is somewhere near here, remember. That's where whoever it is is making for. If we can make it to the hunting lodge and I can contact Berlin, I could still save Beate."

"You sound as if you're feeling better. Your voice is strong again."

"Yes. Help me up."

Ten minutes later they saw the big Opel truck. Again Erika scouted forward. Hellmann waited. He heard her call his name, and there was an edge of panic or horror in her voice that made him half run.

Erika was staring down, wide-eyed, at the two corpses.

"My God, that's the Czech—Stachek," Hellmann said.

"And the other . . . is it . . . is it Wrack?"

"Yes. It must be. How the hell did Stachek get here? He was with the Americans."

Erika turned away. "Wrack must have escaped in the truck."

"Maybe Stachek followed in the jeep."

Erika moved away, toward the path that led out of the clearing and ran dead-straight into the forest. She squatted suddenly.

"There was someone else. He went this way."

Hellmann only half heard her. He had seen something lying in the grass. He picked it up. Wrack's dagger.

"What did you say?"

"There was someone else. It must have been O'Mara."

Hellmann moved toward her and looked down. The footprints were clearly defined.

"He killed Stachek with Wrack's dagger," said Hellmann. "He's making for the lodge. That's all he wanted from the start—a new passport and the money. Let's go."

"We must be careful. O'Mara terrifies me."

"Don't worry. Probably by the time we get there he'll be long gone."

36

Hellmann would have been right if O'Mara had been other than he was: a very, very careful man.

He had found the hunting lodge with ridiculous ease, considering the mystery that Wrack had wrapped round its location.

It was less than a twenty-minute walk from the clearing where he'd halted the truck and where Wrack had died.

It stood on a hill, on its own; it was a natural vantage point. The figure on the veranda was taking full advantage of that fact, raking the countryside with field glasses.

Ninety-nine men out of a hundred would have waved, shouted, run up the hill toward their goal. But O'Mara was the hundredth man. He ducked out of sight and thought hard for several minutes.

Then he began to circle, slowly, carefully, making sure that his movements could not be detected by the watcher above. He surveyed all the ground round the hunting lodge and at last found what he was looking for. A tongue of rough scrub extended up the hill to within a few yards of the back of the house. It was the only way a man could approach the lodge without risk of detection. Even so, a man would have to move with infinite care.

O'Mara did. He went up through the scrub on his belly, moving by inches. By the time he reached the last of the bushes, the sun was beating down out of a cloudless sky, and O'Mara's face and hands were crisscrossed with innumerable scratches from brambles.

Within five paces of the destination he had dreamed of for days, to reach which he had killed God knew how many men, O'Mara waited.

"We'll give them until five o'clock," one twin said to the other. "After that we won't wait any longer. The country-side is probably swarming with Americans as it is."

"But our orders are to kill them."

"I know that. But what the hell does it matter now? If they're not here by five it means that they're probably dead anyway. By tomorrow or the day after there won't be anybody around to check whether we carried out our orders or not."

"You're right," said the other. "It's funny, how old habits die hard."

"I wonder what Bormann will do. And Eichmann. And Kaltenbrunner."

"If I know them, they had their plans laid weeks ago. You mark my words. We'll see the whole bunch of them in Madrid. Keep watch. I'll go and look at the bike. One of her tires is soft—and we don't want a breakdown, do we?"

He went out. The other picked up the field glasses and went to the window.

O'Mara got under cover just in time to watch the squat, crop-haired man walk round to a lean-to extension on the side of the house. The man unhooked the latch and swung open the door. Inside was a motorcycle and sidecar. The man squatted by the rear of the bike and felt the tire. Then he stood up, opened the door of the sidecar, burrowed inside, and brought out a foot-operated pump.

While he fitted the pump to the tire and started to pump, O'Mara was unlacing his boots. He worked deftly and silently. He had heard part of the conversation between the two men in the lodge. His German was primitive; instinct rather than a precise understanding of what they had said had alerted him to the danger.

The squat man finished pumping the tire. He folded up the pump and methodically replaced it in the sidecar. With equal thoroughness he closed the door of the lean-to. Then he walked a few paces away from the lodge, unbuttoning his trousers, and to O'Mara's delight, turned his back and started to urinate.

It had been Murphy, the little old bomb expert, who had taught O'Mara how to make an effective garrote out of bootlaces, string, a necktie, anything at hand. O'Mara's ability to move silently, like a cat, was a natural talent.

The squat man could have known very little about his death. One minute he was emptying his bladder in the sunshine, with a pleasant feeling of relief; the next, there was a band of agony across his throat, his head was being severed from his body, he was in a paralyzing grip from which there was no escape—and then nothing. O'Mara lowered him to the ground very slowly. He didn't want to alert the other man; he wanted his death to be equally swift and silent. But he had not seen the other man; he had no idea that he was an identical twin. Even if he had known, it would not have occurred to him that a telepathy existed between them.

The other man *felt* his twin brother's death. It was a physical sensation as well as a mental intuition, and it

185

came to him just as he was adjusting the dial on the field glasses to bring two figures, emerging from the forest, into focus.

If he had done what O'Mara would have done, if he had crept noiselessly to the opposite window and bided his time, he would have survived. But he didn't. Something—it may even have been grief—made him dash for the door, scooping up his Luger as he went.

He cried out his brother's name as he erupted onto the veranda, and a burst from O'Mara's Garand caught him full in the chest and tossed him, dead, back inside the lodge. But O'Mara wasn't taking any chances. He kicked his way inside the lodge firing burst after burst.

As the echoes of gunfire faded away, Hellmann raised his head cautiously and looked up toward the lodge.

"It's O'Mara," Erika whispered. "I saw the red of his hair. I knew it. I knew he'd get through."

"If the Americans have put out patrols, that firing could bring them here fast. We'd better get a move on."

Erika clutched his arm.

"He'll kill us."

"I don't see why he should."

Her eyes were blazing at him. She gripped his arm. "My God, have you forgotten already? What happened at the farm?"

"But surely he won't—"

"Of course he will."

Her eyes were wild. He'd never seen her like that.

"You hit him. You threatened to have him shot. He'll never forgive you. Don't you understand—can't you see it, even now? He's the worst of them. Wrack was a saint compared to him. He's a killer, a pure killer."

"Then what the hell *do* we do?"

Erika was shivering, in spite of the warmth from the sun.

"We must kill him. It's the only way."

"But I can hardly walk. I couldn't fire straight even if I had a gun."

"There is a way," Erika said. "It worked before."

O'Mara was examining the contents of the suitcase and the cashbox, which he had forced open. The money didn't interest him as much as the blank identity documents, the rubber stamps, the seals. He realized that they represented a fortune. The war would be over in a few days, perhaps a few hours. Germany would be swarming with people desperate for a safe new identity, ready to pay anything for it. He had ready-made contacts in Munich. It would be easy to set up the business. In a few weeks he could make himself rich. Then over the border into Switzerland with a knapsack full of diamonds, gold, and then . . .

He heard the light footsteps on the stony path that led up to the lodge. He whipped up his Garand and crouched by the window. He edged round and looked.

He could hardly believe his eyes—or his luck.

He strode to the door and opened it.

Erika raised her hands instantly.

"Don't shoot," she said. "Please."

"Shoot?" O'Mara said. "Well now, why on earth would I want to do that? Come in, will you. It's snug in here. Just step round that. It's nothing but a dead German who tried to kill me."

He stood aside as Erika entered the lodge.

Erika didn't look at the huddle of blood, clothes, and flesh in the corner.

"Well, of all things," O'Mara said. "Hellmann?"

She drew a finger across her throat. "He's dead," she said in German. "He was hit as he got out of the jeep."

O'Mara seemed to understand.

"Isn't that a shame now," O'Mara said. "You were that fond of him, now, weren't you? *Du—liebe* Hellmann."

She shrugged. Her eyes were dull, expressionless.

"How—you—find—this—place?" O'Mara asked.

She explained, in German, with a few of the English words she knew. O'Mara got the gist of it.

"Well, God love us, you're the little survivor, aren't you?" he said.

"Please," she said, "help me."

As once before, she put her hands on her breasts. But this time she went further. Rapidly, awkwardly, she stripped off her clothes.

O'Mara watched her. He was thinking: Sweet Christ, I can do anything to her. She'll let me do anything I want. Anything I want her to do to me, she'll do it. She has no choice. I'll take her with me. Good cover, a woman. Take her to Munich. When I've finished with her I can sell her . . . or keep her, maybe. Make her work for me. . . .

Erika was naked. She attempted a smile, then took two paces toward the table. She stood in front of it, her back to the open door. Then she bent over, spreading her legs, offering her buttocks.

Hellmann waited until O'Mara's grunts, and the squeaks from the table, were coming regularly. He knew he had to wait for that, had to exercise a final measure of self-control. Like O'Mara he had crawled up to the lodge on his belly, through the scrub. When he'd reached the lodge, he'd signaled to Erika. She had walked openly up the hill.

Now he was by the door, waiting, Wrack's dagger in his hand.

Erika was moaning. He knew he wouldn't be able to stand it much longer. He transferred the dagger to his damaged hand and wiped the sweat from his good hand. Then, gripping the dagger in his good hand, he moved.

It was easy. As easy as it had been the first time, when he'd brought down the butt of his Schmeisser on O'Mara's head. Only this time he wrenched O'Mara's head back, with two fingers in his nostrils, and drew the blade across his throat once, twice, and again.

37

It was just after four o'clock in the afternoon. The sky over Berlin was gray with cloud; dusk was approaching.

The Soviet artillery barrage had intensified during the afternoon. The area round the bunker shook with explosion after explosion. Occasionally shrapnel whined dangerously through the Chancellery garden.

The bodies of Hitler and his wife lay in a shallow trench. The breeze had blown back a corner of the blanket covering Hitler, exposing his feet.

In between barrages, while the Soviet gunners were reloading, two German officers made sorties from the shelter of the bunker entrance and emptied cans of petrol over the bodies.

Hitler had been very precise in his final instructions. He wanted his body, and that of his wife, destroyed without a trace. Accordingly he had ordered that two hundred liters of petrol should be used. But 180 liters were all that had been scrounged, and under the circumstances it was impossible to ensure that all of it was poured onto the bodies.

There was a lull in the bombardment. One of the FBK officers struck a match and threw it onto the gas-soaked blanket that covered Hitler. The match went out. He tried a second time, and a third. Then the shells started landing again, and the two officers scurried for the shelter of the bunker entrance.

There were eight men standing under the concrete canopy: Bormann, Goebbels, Hewel, Axmann, General Rattenhuber, Dr. Stumpfegger, Günsche, and Linge.

It was Linge, ever practical, who thought of a method of igniting Adolf Hitler's funeral pyre. He twisted scraps of paper into spills. He lit the first spill with his cigarette lighter and handed it to Bormann.

Bormann threw it toward the trench. It fell short. Linge handed Bormann another. This time the spill, like a child's paper dart, flew into the trench. A few seconds passed and the trench erupted into blue flame.

Bormann joined the others in raising his arm stiffly in the Hitler salute.

190

As the Soviet guns drummed out Adolf Hitler's funeral march, Bormann reflected that, whatever happened, it would be the last time he raised his arm in the Fascist salute.

38

MAY 1, 1945, 11:00 A.M.

"You were right, Fenner," General Stack said. "If you'd sent out a patrol right away I'd have had your hide. So?"

"So when the patrols did go out, they found the jeep abandoned in the woods, and, further on, the truck with Göring's precious rugs, or whatever, full of bullets. Also two bodies. The Czech and a German, we presume. He'd been shot at close range and there wasn't too much to identify. We think he may have been the SS officer, Wrack, the guy the Czech was gunning for."

"Did Wrack kill the Czech?"

"No, sir. We don't think so. His throat was cut. The patrol went on and found a house, right in the middle of the forest. There was another body there—also with his throat cut. We found the weapon, an SS dagger."

"We have identification of that body, General," Lieutenant Stanton cut in. "A British Corps member.

Actually an Irishman. Sean O'Mara. He was wanted in Ireland before the war—the IRA, you know. We believe he went to Germany in 1939 and asked for political asylum."

"Okay, Stanton, thanks. Anything else, Fenner?"

"Yes, sir. Two more bodies at the house. Both Germans. Funny thing, they were identical twins. One garroted, the other shot. The place was a real butcher's shop. We don't know exactly how the twins fitted in to all this, but we assume that they were there to provide new IDs and the money—according to what the Czech told us."

"Any sign of anything like that?"

"No, sir. Only a radio which got smashed in all the shooting."

"So how many of the bastards does that leave unaccounted for?"

"I'm not exactly sure, sir."

"I think I can help you on that, sir," Stanton said eagerly. "I've had a report in from T section. They found a castle full of dead bodies. One of them we've managed to identify as Thomas Ward and another as Jacques Duval—both British Corps."

"Then there's the guy we got in the village. Legge."

"How many does that leave? Two?"

"One, sir. I think we may have found Chandra, the Anglo-Indian guy, in a river. The report's a little confused—suggests that the dead man is black. But I think it must be our man."

"Then there's just an army guy—Hellmann?"

"And the girl, sir," Fenner added. "We've found no trace of the girl they kidnapped."

"Poor bitch. I guess they raped her, killed her, and buried her somewhere."

"I guess they did."

There was silence for a moment.

"We're still looking for Hellmann, sir," Fenner said.

"Keep looking," said Stack. "But you know, Major, if he got away with a pile of money and a new ID, you've got about as much chance of getting him as Germany has of winning the war."

39

The motorbike and sidecar turned off the narrow, serpentine alpine road into a disused quarry.

Hellmann switched off the motor and Erika climbed stiffly out of the sidecar.

Erika was dressed in a brown skirt and a woolen jersey. Hellmann was wearing old gray slacks, a checked shirt, and a tweed jacket. They had found the clothes in an abandoned farm.

They walked together out of the quarry, Hellmann limping heavily, Erika carrying the suitcase.

"How far is this place?" Hellmann said.

"Across country, perhaps two hours.'

"And you really think your uncle's going to welcome you with open arms?"

"Great-uncle," Erika corrected. "He probably won't remember me. I haven't seen him since I was five or six. But I know we'll be safe there for the time being. At least we'll be in Austria, out of Germany. And don't forget we have money—and we can write out our own identity cards. We've made it, Karl. We've made it."

"I suppose we have." He kissed her. "I can hardly believe it. Four days ago I was in Berlin, in the bunker, in Adolf Hitler's private office. And in between then and now . . ."

"Come on."

They started to walk. After a few moments Erika said: "I once asked you why you carried on when it all seemed so pointless. Before you knew about your sister."

Hellmann winced. He had been unable to contact Berlin. O'Mara had shot up the radio. He had to face the fact that Beate was probably dead.

"Well?" he said.

"You told me that you were trying to purge yourself—something like that."

"Did I? I don't remember."

"Yes, you did. I understood in a way. You fought through the whole war. You were a soldier, like my father. You must have realized—before the Göring mission—that it had all been for nothing."

"I suppose I did. Usually I was too tired or too busy to think much. I didn't really understand the truth until I saw Hitler—saw what he was."

"What was he?"

"He was O'Mara. He was exactly like O'Mara. I knew it in the bunker. I knew he was nothing but a killer. But it wasn't until we got to that castle that I knew the full evil of Hitler. I don't think Germany will ever be forgiven.

I don't see how she can ever be forgiven."

They walked on in silence and suddenly Hellmann laughed. "But do you know the greatest irony? In all my experiences, before the war, during the war, in the last four days, I only ever met one genuine National Socialist."

"Bormann?"

"No. Not Bormann. Bormann was interested in nothing but personal power. Every regime that has ever existed has thrown up its Bormanns. And not Wrack either. Wrack was just a robot, built by Himmler. No. The one real National Socialist I knew was Legge."

"Legge?"

"Yes. Legge."

He laughed again.

"Why do you laugh?" Erika said, taking his arm. "Why do you call it ironical?"

"Simply because," he replied, "Legge was an Englishman."